The Special Prisoner

Also by Jim Lehrer

Books

White Widow

The Last Debate

Purple Dots

Fine Lines

Blue Hearts

A Bus of My Own

Short List

Lost and Found

The Sooner Spy

Crown Oklahoma

Kick the Can

We Were Dreamers

Viva Max!

Plays

The Will and Bart Show

Church Key Charlie Blue

Chili Queen

Jim Lehrer

THE SPECIAL PRISONER

A NOVEL

PublicAffairs

NEW YORK

PublicAffairs books are available at special discounts for bulk purchases
in the U.S. by corporations, institutions, and other organizations. For more
information, please contact the Special Markets Department at
The Perseus Books Group, 11 Cambridge Center, Cambridge MA 02142,
or call (617) 252-5298.

Book Design by Jenny Dossin.

ISBN 1-58648-042-1 (pbk.)
Library of Congress Catalog Number 01-019351

FIRST PUBLICAFFAIRS EDITION 2001

1   3   5   7   9   10   8   6   4   2

For Meg—and James

Now I lay me down to sleep,
I pray the Lord my soul to keep,
If I should die before I wake,
I pray the Lord my soul to take.

I

Hello Again

CHAPTER ONE

Bishop John Quincy Watson, a man of God and grace, was yanked back into his ordeal of hate and horror by a pair of eyes.

They flashed at him from out of the crowd in a concourse at the Dallas–Fort Worth airport—DFW, as it was known by those who knew airports. He stopped with a jolt and turned around. He fixed his sights on the backs of people walking past.

None of the backs looked familiar.

He walked toward Gate 32A, where he was to board a flight to Washington's National Airport.

The bishop hadn't seen the face, only the eyes.

Whose *were* they?

Then he knew. It came to him cleanly, clearly, and absolutely. The eyes were those of a man he knew fifty years ago as "the Hyena." He knew it with a crushing certainty that was as unshakable as John Quincy Watson's faith in the Almighty.

For reasons of exercise and pride, the bishop seldom used the motorized carts provided at airports for the old and lame, choosing instead to make his way slowly on his own

with his ivory-headed cane. He was seventy-one years old
and retired from his post as the Methodist bishop of San Antonio, Texas, but he did not see himself as an old man. Not
yet. He was still active, traveling extensively around the
world as a guest lecturer and preacher. He was on his way,
in fact, to address an ecumenical prayer breakfast at a large
Methodist church in one of Washington's Virginia suburbs.

Now he did raise a hand to hail one of the carts, which
fortunately had no other passengers. He told the young man
driving that he was in a terrific hurry to get to the opposite
end of the concourse.

They beeped their way through the crowd of people and
their various rolling suitcases. "Right here, son," said the
bishop to the cart driver after several minutes. "Let me off
right here, please."

There he was, the man with the eyes. It was him—his
height and build, his bearing and presence. There he was
handing his boarding pass to a female flight attendant at the
gate. There was the man John Quincy Watson would never,
ever forget.

Watson walked as fast as he could, but the man was down
the boarding corridor and out of sight by the time the slow-
moving bishop reached the flight attendant. He ignored the
other passengers in line and went right up and asked, "Was
that man's name Tashimoto?"

The flight attendant, a fortyish woman with short brown
hair, looked at him as if he were a potential bomber or
masher. But after a second or two of further inspection she
must have concluded he was safe because she looked down at
the stack of tickets on the stand in front of her. "Yes, that's
what it says on the ticket—T-a-s-h-i-m-o-t-o," she said.
"Now, if you'll move out the way, sir, so we can resume
boarding?"

Bishop Watson said, "Where is this plane going, please?"

"To San Diego," she said, pointing to an electric sign near the door that said just that.

"I'd like a ticket, please."

"We're already overbooked, but see the agent at the counter."

The agent confirmed that there were no seats on the plane, and Watson couldn't convince him or the attendant at the gate to let him on for just a few minutes to simply look at the passengers. He told them that he saw a man board whom he had known many years ago.

Against the rules, they said. Permission denied.

In a few minutes the boarding door was closed. Bishop Watson stayed right there and watched through the large plate-glass window as the plane—he recognized it as a Boeing 757—backed out from the gate. Now and then he had wondered what it would be like to fly one of these jetliners compared with *Big Red,* his B-29, and the other propeller planes he had flown in World War II. But it was only an occasional wonder. In fifty years he had never even entered the cockpit of any kind of airplane.

By the time he started walking again toward Gate 32A, he realized that it was already ten minutes past the departure time of his flight.

It didn't matter. The Hyena was *alive*! The little Jap was here in America, on a plane for San Diego!

Bishop Watson felt shame for thinking of the Hyena as a Jap. But it was an unavoidable reflex. For the bishop, this man could never be anything but a Jap.

CHAPTER TWO

Watson had never wanted to be a pilot and did not join the U.S. Army to become one.

It was fourteen months after Pearl Harbor, and he simply could not stand one more day being what he was—a physically fit eighteen-year-old American male who was sitting out the Second World War as a college student in Massachusetts. His parents and almost everyone else said if he waited awhile, at least till the end of his third year at Amherst, he would stand a chance of getting a higher rank and better assignment when he did sign up. But he ignored all such advice, and on February 16, 1943, he took a Peter Pan bus into Springfield and enlisted. He was sent to a base at Haverhill two hours away, where he was given a haircut, an extensive physical, some uniforms, and many written and oral tests.

The army needs pilots, said a captain after three days. You did great on all of the exams relevant to flying, and they've lowered the age and education requirements, so it's off to Texas for you, young man.

Watson figured he could have protested but assumed it would have done no good. Besides, why not be a pilot? He had seen enough movies and photos in newspapers to have a passing and admiring knowledge of the cocky men of the U.S. Army Air Corps in their fur-trimmed flight jackets, goggle sunglasses, and song vow to "live in fame or go down in flames."

Watson had yet to learn how to drive a car, but so what—why not start with driving airplanes?

A flight surgeon told him later that only people who feel invincible and who are turned on by speed can be really good pilots. Watson was stunned to find that he took to flying about as naturally as a bird. He had an affinity and talent—an instinct, really—for it. He had no idea where it came from or why, but he had it. He found something superhuman—supernatural even—about racing a piece of machinery down a runway and getting the thing up into the air. Each takeoff gave him an enormous feeling of accomplishment and well-being—and the urge to shout like a show-off child: *Look at me, world! I'm a bird, I'm a plane, I'm Superman!*

There was something even more exhilarating about actually being up there in the sky with the birds and the gods, sharing with them the clouds and a spectacular view of rivers, mountains, forests, deserts, and plains as well as the structures and signs of human life, our highways and roads, our cities and towns.

Watson also cherished the quiet and the freedom up there, the sensation of floating and then whipping and zipping through space, of being alone, of being untouchable and—invincible. He even got a kick out of dodging lightning, thunder, and crazy winds and landing planes in trouble, motors out or sputtering or on fire, flaps stuck, wheels locked, instruments shot, radio contact lost. He loved it all.

Watson graduated first in his class every step of his training and thus expected to go to fighters, where the best were usually assigned. But then one afternoon, in a closed and guarded Quonset building at a mud hole of an airfield in southeastern Kansas, a major told him he was going first to Big Spring, Texas, and then back to another base in Kansas to learn to fly bombers and eventually the big new plane that was going to win the war—the B-29 Superfortress. The major said it was just as well Watson was going to bombers because "at your height, Watson, you'd have a problem fitting into a fighter anyhow."

He also presented Watson something he gave every pilot chosen for bomber duty. It was a written statement from a General Grant—David, not Ulysses—who was the top Army Air Forces medical officer in Europe. It was what Grant told all his doctors as a way of getting them to understand, from their office chairs, what it was like to deal in combat with the 130 controls, switches, levers, dials, and gauges in the cockpit of a B-17 Flying Fortress, the main predecessor of the B-29:

> Cut the size of your office to a five-foot cube, engulf it in the roar of four 1,000-horsepower engines, increase your height above the ground to four or five miles, reduce the atmospheric pressure by one half to two thirds, lower the outside temperature to forty to fifty below zero. That will give you an idea of the *normal* conditions under which the pilots, navigators, and bombardiers must work out the higher mathematical relationships of engine revolutions, manifold and fuel pressure, aerodynamics, barometric pressure, wind drift, air speed, ground speed, position, direction, and plane attitude.
>
> As the final touch to this bizarre picture of intense concentration amid intense distraction, add the fear of death.

·   ·   ·

Death.
Died. Killed. Deceased. Gone. Missing. Mangled. Burned.

Incinerated. Those words quickly became the words of John Quincy Watson's new world as an eighteen-year-old cadet in the United States Army Air Forces.

His first death: He had awakened at 0530 in the bunk next to Amos Werth of Schenectady, New York. By lights-out that night, Werth's bunk was empty and his gear was gone. He had lost his bearings during an easy practice flight, panicked, and crashed into a concrete farm silo near Clare-more, Oklahoma, fifty miles south of their primary training base at Coffeyville, Kansas. The speculation was that he must have frozen with his hands hard on the stick. Watson had barely known Werth, which in some ways made it even worse. There he was and there he wasn't. Werth had been a philosophy major at Penn State—that was about all Watson knew about him.

Watson didn't remember even that much about the two others killed before he left Coffeyville. One died of a broken neck when his plane crashed into a tree after a bad takeoff; the other died while trying to make an emergency landing on a small blacktop road near a Kansas town called Cherryvale. That was the death Watson remembered most vividly. The guy hit some telephone poles and electrical wires on the way down; the crash set off an explosion and a fire that got so hot it burned a huge hole in the blacktop and transformed the pilot cadet into a small pile of ashes.

Their senior flight instructor, a major who had won the Distinguished Flying Cross and five Air Medals flying fighters in Europe, took Watson and the other cadets over in a truck to see the crash site. He made them get out and walk to the exact spot on the blacktop where the pilot—their late classmate—had been incinerated. The remains of the man had been removed, but there was a large, dark greasy spot— about the size of a man—burned into the roadway.

"He did not pay attention to the basics," said the major.

"He did not have to die—he could have easily landed that plane on this road if he had kept his wits and skills about him." Then he pointed right at the spot in the melted road and said, "The lesson, gentlemen, is that in our business, this is what you look like if you make a mistake."

Neither those words nor that greasy spot discouraged Watson from wanting to be a pilot. By then, nothing could have. What he thought about on the truck ride back to Coffeyville was how *he* would have easily maneuvered that plane to a safe landing.

·   ·   ·

Watson had heard about the B-29 Superfortress and some of its test and training flights that had not gone so well. News like that travels from pilot to pilot as fast as the wind blows. The biggest tragedy was the death of Eddie Allen, Boeing's famous test pilot, on the B-29's second test flight. The plane caught fire and crashed into a meat-packing house near downtown Seattle, killing Allen and his crew plus nineteen people on the ground.

It had been common knowledge since then that B-29s were being built and put into the sky at such an accelerated pace that a lot of people were going to crash into a lot of packing plants and create a lot of greasy spots before the big machines ended the war.

So be it, thought Watson. *So be it.* That was his attitude and his eighteen-year-old life at that moment.

The Smoky Hill Army Airfield near Salina, up in central Kansas, was one of the main training bases for B-29 crews. Up till now, they said the day Watson arrived, the B-29 pilots who had gone to India, China, and the newly captured Pacific-island bases were mostly experienced, having flown smaller bombers in Europe and Africa. Watson's class was the first to go directly from training to flying the big birds.

The U.S. Army Air Forces had no choice but to use green-horns, they said, because they had run out of the other kind.

Unsaid, of course, was the reason: They'd died.

They called the B-29 the largest bomber in the world, and from the outside it was. But General Grant was right about it being cramped inside. The bombardier was right down there in front exposed to everything. Watson couldn't figure how a guy could sit there without feeling like he was going to fall out. The flight engineer's seat was tight behind the pilot and copilot, the radio operator behind him, with more equipment than Watson thought possible to stick into an airplane. The space was so tiny that the navigator's desk, on the left, across from the radio guy, was on hinges so it could be raised for people to squeeze by.

The first time Watson went inside, on day one of orientation, he sat in the pilot and copilot's seats there in the glass-covered cockpit everybody called "the greenhouse." Then he crawled on his hands and knees through a tunnel, full of cables and oxygen lines, that ran above the bomb bays to the midsection gunners' compartment. Those gunners' windows —they called them blisters—didn't look that strong. Watson sat in "the barber's chair," a swivel seat where the top gunner perched to see enemy aircraft coming from overhead and sight the guns by remote control. Back in the tail was the rear gunner compartment, with barely enough room for one man, the poor bastard.

Then they fired up the engines and taxied around in circles a few times. The instructor at the controls in the greenhouse was a captain named Richardson, who'd flown thirty-five missions in B-17s for the Eighth Air Force out of England before being switched to B-29s. He was thirty-two years old, and that made him an old man to Watson's crowd. None of them ever asked him about Europe, but Watson heard that the captain had lost his best friend, who was his copilot, when a Nazi plane sprayed machine-gun fire into the air-craft, tearing holes through the copilot's flak jacket and splattering blood and bits of flesh all over Richardson and the cockpit. Richardson completed the bombing mission over a steel plant in Germany and returned to the base in England with what was left of his dead friend strapped there in the seat next to him. They gave him the Silver Star.

Watson wondered if he would win any medals before this was over. He assumed he would.

·   ·   ·

The day before Watson actually flew a B-29 for the first time happened to be November 14, his nineteenth birthday, and he mentioned that to another pilot, Joey Smith, who had come to Smoky Hill with him. Smith, who was from some small town in Mississippi, had turned twenty-three a couple of weeks earlier, so the two took a shuttle bus into Salina to see if there was something there to do to celebrate their birthdays. There wasn't. After a few minutes of walking around, they were both ready to get back to Smoky Hill. There was still much to do to be ready for tomorrow.

They went into the drugstore next to the bus station to look at some magazines while they waited for the next bus back. A clerk, a fairly good-looking blond woman in her thirties, asked if they were stationed out at Smoky Hill.

"We sure are, ma'am," said Joey.

"Well, everybody here in town sees those big Boeing bombers flying overhead all of the time, but nobody knows for sure anything about what's going on. The *Salina Journal* never has any stories. Every time anybody asks about it we're told it's all top secret. Is that right?"

"That's right," Watson said.

"Is it true Hitler's being held prisoner out there?"

"Top secret," Joey said.

"How about that Jap leader, Tōjō?"

"Top secret," Watson said.

"Where you boys from?"

"Top secret," Joey drawled.

"Casablanca," Watson said. Telling that lie was his only act of celebration.

.   .   .

Watson and crew were rousted at 0400 the next morning and given a special breakfast of steak and eggs and biscuits and lots of coffee. There was a short briefing and then a truck ride to the plane out on the runway. It had been cold every day Watson had been at Smoky Hill, and it was cold again this morning.

They lined up in front of the plane, and with Captain Richardson watching, Watson inspected all ten members of his crew. He checked to make sure each had a parachute and cold-weather flying gear, a flight helmet, an oxygen mask, a headset and microphone for the intercom, a life vest, goggles, and sunglasses, among other things. He gave a thumbs-up to Richardson and said to the crew, "Okay, let's go."

Everything in precheck went fine. The weather was clear; the sun was coming up. Visibility was good. But takeoff was the single most dangerous time with any plane, and the more sophisticated the aircraft, the more there is that can go wrong. The key was always to know when to abort take-off—to be able to be rolling down the runway and know that the speed isn't right, the feel isn't right, to get a clean liftoff and to abort in time to keep from crashing off the end.

They started to taxi.

Watson's plane was fourth in line on the runway behind Joey Smith's. As soon as Joey was gone, Watson moved up, came to a full stop, goosed the power. The flight engineer gave the thumbs-up, Watson released the brakes, gunned it full-throttle, and tore off down the runway. He had to have at least 90 knots of speed when he got to the control tower on the left—or forget it and put on the brake. As the plane rolled, he asked the side gunners if they saw smoke coming out of any of the engines. Negative. Anything on fire? Negative. Speed went up to 40 knots . . . 50 . . . 60. The control tower was coming. Now he was at 75 knots . . . 80 . . . 90 . . . 95. No stopping now. He was one minute and five seconds into the roll, speed 140 knots.

Then he heard an excited voice from the control tower say: "Watch out! Emergency ahead!"

Watson had no choice but to keep going. It was too late to abort. He pulled up the control column, and the plane left the ground. The copilot immediately hit the wheels-up switch. Just ahead Watson saw the emergency. Joey Smith's plane was down and burning in a field. There was fire and smoke, and then, right below them, an explosion. The fuel tanks must have blown. Watson kept the control column up. He was at 200 knots. He and his plane and crew were safe. They were gone.

There was no way to tell if Joey or any of his crew survived. Watson asked his tail gunner if he could see any sign of life back down there. Negative, the gunner came back. He asked everyone on the intercom if they were all right. One at a time, each answered yes, sir.

Watson had a good, uneventful flight, and when he returned to base two hours and five minutes later, Joey's plane was still there, smoldering and smoking. Nobody knew what had happened. It seemed that one engine had caught fire and then another, and the plane had gone down seconds after it left the ground. Everybody on board had died. Watson knew them all. Joey's copilot was from California and his father was the leader of a dance band Watson remembered hearing on the radio once or twice.

The bodies were taken away in ambulances while Watson's plane was in the air. He wondered where they put them. Had the U.S. Army Air Forces made an arrangement with a mortuary in Salina to handle dead bodies in groups of eleven?

Watson reminded himself of what pilots had to believe about going down in a plane: At least you die doing something you want to do, something that matters. Who in the hell wants to live long enough to die of cancer or a heart attack if you can go down in flames in an airplane?

Five planes and twenty-one crewmen were lost in various mechanically driven accidents during the ten weeks he was at Smoky Hill and at Herington, the Kansas town east of Salina that was the final staging area.

And that was before Japs started shooting at them.

.   .   .

The possibility of being shot at—and down—was not completely ignored. There were intelligence briefings on being captured as well as many hours of training on ditching and crash landing.

The briefings were conducted by an older major, a calm man who smoked a pipe and needed a haircut. If captured, he said, expect the worst because the worst was what all American prisoners had received from the Japanese since the beginning of the war. They acted against Americans like deranged butchers, savages from an alien culture, he said, rather than as soldiers from a civilized world. He said the Japanese signed the Geneva convention, but it was never ratified by the government. Shortly after the war started, a Japanese official said they would abide by the agreement, but they seldom—if ever—did.

The worst of the Japanese's behavior, regrettably, said the major, was toward the flyers—"special prisoners," they were called—because the Japanese considered them officially war criminals, not soldiers. He said their parliament or prime minister or somebody actually made that the law of their land after the famous Doolittle raid over Tokyo in 1942. If captured, the flyers should expect to be humiliated, starved, beaten, tortured, maimed, mutilated, and, most regrettably, in some cases, even killed. No trials, no orders from higher command were necessary. Their favorite means of executing captured American flyers was chopping off their heads.

The major then said, looking right at Watson: "For reasons that are still not clear, our information is that Americans with red hair are particularly enraging to the Japanese. So to you, Lieutenant, I would offer words of special and extreme caution."

John Quincy Watson thanked the major for his concern, but his newly acquired arrogance and self-confidence as a pilot were such that he dismissed it as irrelevant.

Nobody was ever going to shoot *him* down.

CHAPTER THREE

There were no Tashimotos listed in the white pages of the San Diego telephone book. And no one at the American Airlines counters at the San Diego airport remembered seeing anyone who answered the rough description that the old man with a cane offered in his slow search for what he said was a "misplaced business associate" who was to have changed planes here.

The bishop was an hour and forty-five minutes behind the man he thought was the Hyena, having caught the next plane from DFW to San Diego. He figured there were three possible reasons for the Hyena's going to San Diego: He was on a business or personal visit, he lived there and was returning home, or he was only stopping there on his way to another destination—by another plane or by car.

Bishop John Quincy Watson believed that God, in His wisdom, really did have a will that He worked regularly and often in mysterious ways. So he went about his labors in San Diego with a sense that whatever was meant to be would be. A conclusion would eventually reveal itself. Either he would locate the man he believed to be the Hyena and deal with him, or he would not. Joyce had often accused her husband of being a fatalist, and he conceded that the line between a believer and a fatalist was sometimes hard to find. He had even devoted a major sermon to the subject, making the point that believers, unlike fatalists, know, accept, and celebrate the fact that God has a hand in whatever happens.

God, in His wisdom, chose the yellow pages as His revealing instrument this time. Bishop Watson called the leading hotels, asking each if Mr. Tashimoto had checked in. He couldn't remember the Hyena's first name or even if he'd ever known it. An operator at the Hotel Bayfront replied in the affirmative about a Tashimoto being registered. Watson quickly hung up before being asked if he wanted to be connected, and after a fifteen-minute taxi ride he was seated in the Bayfront lobby.

Watson, as a way of thinking matters through, often spoke out loud to himself, and he felt a strong need to do so now. But that was clearly not an option. The lobby was huge and busy, and one of his self-addresses, no matter how muted he kept his voice, would no doubt draw unwanted attention.

There was nothing to do but act. He rose slowly and carefully from the lobby chair and went to a house phone.

He asked to be connected to Mr. Tashimoto's room.

On the third ring the phone was answered.

"Hello," said a man.

Watson did not reply.

"Is somebody on this line?" said the man. "Who are you calling?"

You, fucky duck, is what Bishop John Quincy Watson wanted very much to say.

But he said nothing and hung up the phone.

There was no question in his mind that the man he had just heard was the Hyena. Fifty years of passing time—fifty years and eight months, to be exact—could age but not change the high-pitched preciseness of that awful voice.

He went to the front desk and told a young female room clerk that he was there for a reunion with Mr. Tashimoto, whom he had not seen since "our days together in World War II."

"How about helping me surprise him with a knock on the door?" Watson asked. "Could you give me his room number, please?"

"I'm sorry, but that's against policy. Safety and privacy— you know how it is, sir."

He lowered his eyes and shook his head in sadness and disappointment. She relented, clearly being unable to resist cheering up this sincere and obviously harmless and distinguished elderly gentleman.

"Mr. Tashimoto's room is 1808," she said quietly.

Watson figured that the tiny sterling silver cross he wore in his suitcoat's left lapel may have also been helpful. It usually was.

.   .   .

John Quincy Watson knocked on the door of room 1808. There was no response, so he knocked a second time and, after several moments of silence, a third. Then he put his good ear— the right one—to the door and soon heard what he thought was the sound of a toilet flushing and then water running.

Watson had a disturbing vision of the Hyena relieving himself and then washing his hands in the bathroom of a luxury hotel room in the United States of America.

He knocked one more time.

Within seconds the door opened but only the few inches permitted by the chain that remained in place on the other side of the door.

Watson, a very tall man, looked down just above the extended chain at two eyes blasting out at him like two dark brown lasers.

"Hello again," John Quincy Watson said to the eyes.

"What may I do for you?" said the man in a subdued voice. But his screech was down in there. Watson could hear it.

"My name is Watson. We were together in the war."

"I have no recollection of you."

"I recognized you from your eyes."

"What do you want to talk to me about?"

"Nothing in particular really."

"Then, please, not now. I am about to go to dinner."

"A few minutes for old times' sake?"

Watson stepped back as the door jerked shut. Was the Hyena going to let him in? Watson had no plan; if the man refused to engage, then there was nothing else to do but go back to the airport and get on the next plane to Washington.

The door opened.

"I do not know you, but if you wish to talk for a moment, we can do so," said the elderly man.

Watson's natural instinct was to offer his right hand. But the other man kept his on the doorknob, his left by his side. A Western-style handshake was definitely not what he had in mind. So Watson kept his own right hand on his cane as he stepped into the room.

"Hello again, hello again," Watson said once the door was closed behind them.

The man said, "I do not know you, so it cannot be again that we meet."

Watson took a good look at this man standing in front of him all dressed up in a light gray suit, white dress shirt, and yellow-and-black striped tie. He was about five feet three, with the same slight build and olive skin Watson remembered. The Hyena's head had been completely shaved then, his eyebrows full and black. Now his hair and eyebrows were thin and silver. Watson's own hair had been curly and red fifty years ago and was now almost nonexistent except for a few reddish white strands across the top and patches around the ears.

The room, known as an executive suite in luxury-hotel parlance, was spacious and well-appointed. There was a sizable writing desk in a separate sitting area furnished with a couch, two overstuffed chairs, and a coffee table. Everything, including the paintings of flowers and hunting dogs on the walls, was first-rate and tasteful. The view out onto San Diego Bay was beautiful.

Watson made his way to the couch, exaggerating the fifty-year-old limp in his right leg. He sat down with great effort and care. Then he said, "You knew me also by a number—345C."

"Where did I know you, please?" said the other man, as he sat down easily in one of the chairs across from Watson.

"At Camp Sengei 4."

"I was never there."

"You were the chief interrogator. You spoke English better than most of us then, and you still do."

"I was never there."

"It was fifty years ago."

"I was never there."

"Say 'fucky duck.' "

"I don't say such things."

"Look at my face closely."

The man did as he was told. For a count of ten, twenty, thirty, and finally for a full minute he stared at the aged, tanned face of John Quincy Watson, moving his focus from the heavily wrinkled forehead to the medium-sized nose, from the narrow chin to the bushy gray eyebrows, from one blue eye to the other.

"I don't know you," he said easily, forthrightly, when he was finished.

"Not even my eyes?" Watson said, opening his blue eyes wide and leaning forward. "I know *your* eyes."

"I recognize nothing about you." The man stood. "Please leave my room, sir."

"I forgave you long ago," said Watson.

"I have never done anything to you." The Japanese man remained standing rigidly, defiantly.

"You were a terrible man, possibly one of the worst God ever put on the face of this earth."

"I am a wonderful man."

CHAPTER FOUR

It was 11:52 P.M., Tokyo time, according to the chronometer on the instrument panel.

They were approaching their primary target, a section of Tokyo that, like all others, was full of buildings—houses, schools, hospitals, stores—and people, presumably mostly women, children, and men too old or infirm to be soldiers of the Rising Sun.

What First Lieutenant John Quincy Watson, commanding his plane, saw from five thousand feet through the night sky full of smoke was a huge X outlined in fire down below. It had been made by a group of four B-29s that went before, dropping incendiary bombs as target markers.

Then, as the first planes in the sortie dropped their loads, also incendiaries, everything was lit up like broad daylight.

An awful smell rushed in with the heat through the open bomb-bay doors. Watson knew it was the odor of Japanese women, children, and old men burning. He also thought he heard screams from down there, but that was truly crazy.

This was his seventeenth mission over Japan. He thoroughly enjoyed the piloting, the challenge of finding the target and threading through flak and enemy-aircraft fire, but for him, that was the extent of the thrills. He appreciated the smartness of the generals in switching them and their B-29s from daylight high-altitude explosive bombing to low-altitude firebombing at night. He knew that incinerating people, places, and things was necessary to end the war. But he had begun to grow uncomfortable, tired of being one of those doing it—night after night after night. He hadn't said a word about this to anyone and had no intention of doing so. They were his private thoughts and nobody else's business.

The squadron chaplain had blessed this mission as he had all others. "Dear Father, let these brave men do their duty for their country and return to do it again and again," he had said at the end of the briefing. The chaplain was an overweight man in his early thirties, an Army Air Forces captain who was a Presbyterian preacher in civilian life. Watson had exchanged no more than a dozen words and no private thoughts with him.

Malone, the radar operator, said the target was thirty seconds away. Watson told Parish, the bombardier, to get ready. Parish switched on the Norden bombsight, confirmed the bomb-bay doors were open. The smoke cleared for a second. Watson could see ground and some fire below.

Parish said the Norden was set. Malone ordered the plane's direction moved two degrees to the right. The smoke thickened again. Watson couldn't see anything. The smell, worse than usual, was seeping through his oxygen mask. The heat was bacon-frying hot. Malone said the slant to the target—he was keying on a group of buildings described by the briefers as "industrial"—was twenty-six degrees. Watson adjusted it to twenty-eight.

Parish said he couldn't see anything down there. His voice was high, tight as it always was at this particular moment in a run. Malone said the radar showed the target was only ten seconds away. Slant now at thirty degrees. Turn one more degree to the right, Malone said. Watson relayed that to Parish, who fed it into the Norden.

"Ready now," Watson said.

Parish, in a near-whisper, repeated that: "Ready now."

For a split second there was a break in the smoke. A city of buildings and people clearly did exist down there.

"Ready now," Watson said again.

"I can't see anything," Parish said.

"Drop 'em," Watson said.

"Bombs away," Parish whispered.

Parish said he could see through the bombsight that his bombs were hitting something, burning, incinerating something.

Watson wondered what those Jap people down there must be thinking; he tried to imagine what it must be like for them, looking up and seeing these big silver airplanes come out of nowhere in the middle of the night and dropping bombs of fire down on them. It was hard to picture completely because Watson had never seen a Jap in person. All he knew from photographs and movies was that they were little, yellow, vicious, and had slanted eyes.

"Let's take *Big Red* home," Watson said on the intercom. His voice sounded reedy, spent—just the way he felt.

Big Red. Naming these planes was a big deal for bomber crews. Most of the names had to do with sex and naked women, but Owens, their navigator, was a happily married Baptist who didn't want to fly a plane with something "obscene" on its nose. He said he wouldn't ever be able to send his wife photographs of him standing, for instance, in front of two huge boobs. They settled on naming the plane *Big Red* after Watson, their command pilot. On the left side of the plane's nose a ground crewman on the island of Saipan had painted the pinup replica of a very redheaded, very bosomy Betty Grable look-alike dressed only in a skimpy, very red two-piece bathing suit. Owens didn't like it, but he was outvoted.

Watson turned the plane away from the glow and the heat and the stench toward Saipan, the island in the Marianas fifteen hundred miles east of Japan where they were based. Their load of five-hundred-pound M-69 incendiaries was rigged in clusters of thirty-eight to explode at two thousand feet and rain fire down over an area roughly sixteen acres.

He felt the hit. It knocked the plane hard to port.

On the intercom, Southie, the copilot, yelled, "A Jap rammed us! A Jap Nick!" A Nick was a two-engine Japanese fighter plane.

Malone shouted, "Big hole in starboard side. Clark's gone. Ozzie's gone." Clark was the starboard-side gunner, Ozzie York the top gunner.

"Gone?" Watson gasped.

"Sucked out—gone," said Malone. At that moment the plane pitched over to the starboard side. Watson asked Malone if he was okay. There was no answer. Had be been sucked out into the atmosphere? Was he now gone, too?

The cockpit was full of smoke—*Big Red*'s smoke. She was lurching back and forth and downward at a high speed. Nothing Watson grabbed, turned, touched, jerked, jammed, or hit changed anything.

This cannot be happening, he thought. Not to me.

Neither ditching in water nor crash-landing on ground was even an option. That training had been a waste of time.

"Bail out!" he shouted into the intercom, not knowing how many of his crew were still aboard, alive, or able to hear it.

Southie gave a thumbs-up and disappeared toward the forward bomb-bay doors, which were behind Watson. Through those doors—thank God they were still open from the bomb run—was the primary way out for those in the front of the plane. The only alternative was to go out through the front wheel housing, but that was closed because the wheel was up.

In a few seconds Parish, the bombardier, came up through the smoke from his position down in the nose. He squeezed by Watson toward the bomb bay.

Watson tried to keep the plane steady, but it was impossible. It was shaking violently. He had flight goggles on, but the smoke was so heavy he could no longer read the instruments. But he didn't need an altimeter reading to know he had only a few minutes before the plane would hit something—some Jap ground or water just off Jap ground.

They had had instruction in using parachutes, but they hadn't actually practiced doing it very much. Most pilots, Watson definitely included, saw fooling with parachutes as the work of the psychologically defeated. The B-29 Superfortress was to be flown and landed, not abandoned.

But if he did not abandon this plane right now, he was surely going to die.

He unbuckled his seat belt and began crawling toward the bomb-bay doors. He uttered some words of thanks to *Big Red* for getting him and his crew safely through the first sixteen missions. Good job, *Big Red,* he said. So long and good luck.

Otherwise, his thoughts during those several seconds on his hands and knees were rather ordinary. He was pretty sure that he was going to die—to become a greasy spot—but at least when it happened he would be able to mutter something up toward heaven about having given survival his best shot. *I didn't give up, I tried to live. And I kept the plane in the air long enough for my crew—those still alive—to bail out.*

Good for you, Quincy Watson, he heard somebody say in a deep male voice.

He saw his mom and dad receiving the news of the heroic death of their tall, redheaded son, and he watched them cry proudly.

He remembered a comedian at the Smoky Hill parachute shed, a master sergeant with a New Jersey accent, who got a huge laugh out of telling everyone to return any parachute that didn't open—there was a money-back guarantee. It had seemed funny at the time.

He was at the bomb bay. He felt the sudden need to say a prayer and had only two to choose from—the Lord's Prayer and one he'd said at bedtime when he was a kid. He chose the shorter one. But he only got out the first line: "Now I lay me down to sleep . . ."

Then he jumped headfirst, down and out.

He saw lights from the ground coming at him. He pulled the parachute rip cord and then remembered a warning in class and in the handbooks: Make sure you're clear of the plane before pulling the cord. Otherwise, you'll get the parachute caught on something and there you'll be—dragged down to your death by your own plane.

The chute popped opened as he fell safely away.

Where had his plane gone? He couldn't find *Big Red* in the sky or any sign of it having crashed down below. Could it have just kept flying on its own toward Saipan?

The air was cool and smelled almost sweet. Watson had no idea where he was, where he was coming down. He figured it had to be somewhere in Japan, but it sure as hell wasn't Tokyo, a portion of which his sortie of 124 B-29s had just set afire like it was a city made of paper. There was no way to know how far from Tokyo he was, but he did catch a glimpse of light across the horizon, way off to his right. Could that be the fires of the city?

There were a few regular lights directly below. It was definitely ground down there, not water. At about five hundred feet, he could see that the lights were moving. Lanterns, flashlights, cars, he concluded. Farther away there were other lights, larger and steady, apparently from houses or other structures.

He was almost down. He pulled at the cords the way the book said to in order to ease the impact of his body landing feet first. His feet hit, and he heard and felt water splashing. He fell forward and realized he was in some kind of field. The sweet smell overhead was now replaced by the odor of manure. He was in a farmer's field, a rice paddy, most probably. But he was alive and conscious and, as best as he could tell, uninjured.

He unbuckled the parachute harness and looked around as moving lights came toward him.

He felt for the loaded .45 pistol that was supposed to be in a holster on his right hip. It was still there. He had fired it at various practice ranges, maybe a dozen times. He had become a fairly good shot, but he was hardly a proficient user of firearms. Watson was a pilot.

What might he do with a loaded pistol here in the dark in the middle of a rice paddy somewhere in Japan with numerous persons unknown bearing down on him?

Should he just surrender? How do you do that? He'd never had a class called How to Surrender to the Japs.

He heard some noise behind him and turned around in time to catch a knockout blow to the side of his head.

·   ·   ·

It was daytime when he came to. The first thing he realized was that he had a really bad headache, as if hammers were crashing in sync against both sides of his head. The second was that he was sore all over from somebody or something hitting him repeatedly. The third was that he was tied, hands and feet, to a post.

A group of tiny people stood around him, chattering at one another, yelling in a language that he assumed was Japanese. They were poorly dressed civilian men and women of all ages—yes, their eyes were slanted, though they didn't look especially yellow—who seemed terribly angry.

One of the women let out a scream at the sight of Watson's opened eyes. She hit him in the stomach with something that felt like the end of a wooden pole or handle. Nothing in Watson's life had ever hurt him that badly. He closed his eyes and discovered that the blow had caused him to both pee and defecate all over himself. Through his pain, he began to sincerely wish he had stayed with *Big Red* and died a quick and honorable death.

The Jap men and women—the women were particularly enthusiastic—continued to take their whacks, each accompanied by an angry shout. He was pummeled in the ribs, face, and chest, in the legs and knees, in the back. So, yes, they were not only little and slant-eyed, they were also vicious.

Drifting in and out of consciousness, Watson had no idea how long the beating went on. His next clear memory was of being on his knees with his hands tied together behind him and a rope hanging like a lasso around his neck. On each side of him was another American, dressed like him, on his knees like him, tied up and beaten like him. He didn't recognize either from his own crew or squadron, but he assumed they were from other B-29s—maybe even from the same mission.

They were lined up on a narrow dirt road in front of a tiny green military truck and four men in uniforms Watson recognized from intelligence briefings as those of the Imperial Army of Japan. The uniforms were light green and brown; their belts and boots were brown.

One soldier, presumably an officer, was clearly in charge.

He had the face and movements of a rat, and he had a problem of some kind. With an occasional word of English and a lot of grunting and pointing and phony smiling, he laid out the dilemma as too many people for his little truck. He kept holding up two fingers. Two prisoners? Two problems? Two *what*?

Then he pointed at the American on Watson's left and shouted something at one of the other Japanese soldiers, who came over to the designated American. The soldier, who looked about Watson's age, bayoneted the American, in a series of sharp, efficient strokes, in the stomach, in the chest, then in the groin and again in the stomach. It happened so swiftly, the American didn't have time to scream or moan. He silently fell forward onto the ground. Watson wondered if he also wished he had gone down with his plane. Where was he from? How old was he? What was the nickname of his plane? Did he have a wife or a mother or a girlfriend? Did he love anybody?

Some of his blood splattered onto Watson's chin and neck and the collar of his flight suit.

The little rat Jap in charge walked over to Watson. He was next, he was number two. That was okay with Watson. He didn't know how that other guy felt, but he wanted to tell the little rat Jap that killing him would be just fine, a blessing really. *Thank you, little rat Jap, for putting me out of this misery. I am from Westbrook, Connecticut. I was a junior at Amherst majoring in business. I have a mother and a father but no steady girlfriend. I will be twenty years old next month, and I'm still a virgin, believe it or not. See you in hell, little rat Jap!*

But the Jap only stuck Watson's own pistol in his face and said, "You gun. Watch."

He rammed the butt of the .45 to the temple of the man on Watson's right and fired. The *pow* jarred Watson as much as the whacks the Jap civilians had taken on him earlier.

The second American, again without crying out, fell forward onto the ground. *Who were* you? *Name, rank, serial number, hometown, airplane name, loves, hates? Did you want to die?*

Again Watson felt the spraying blood. Some got into his right ear and on his right cheek and in his hair. His mind began to race.

Okay, here we go. Now it really is my turn. He closed his eyes and waited. *Will he shoot me with my own pistol or bayonet me? Or maybe cut off my head? The intelligence major at Smoky Hill had said the Japanese liked to behead people like us. Will they do it with a sword or a hatchet? How do they get their sword blades sharp enough to slash through a guy's neck? Will it hurt, or won't I feel it? Will I also go without a sound? Will there be time to scream or holler or yell Fuck you, you little Jap rat! What if the whack doesn't go all the way through and my head is left dangling there? What if it does go through cleanly and there'll be my head just lying there on the ground? Will my eyes be open or closed? What will they do with my head? Or the rest of me, for that matter? Bury it all together? Burn it all together? Leave it here by the side of the road for dogs and crows to eat? It, my body.*

Watson tried to think of something religious to grab onto, tried to remember something from what the chaplain had said. Nothing came. So he did the bedtime prayer again and then remembered a song from Sunday school. "Jesus loves me, this I know, for the Bible tells me so . . ."

He felt a hand in his hair. It belonged to the little rat Jap in charge. He pulled on Watson's hair as he said, "Red. They like. We go."

Then somebody tied a thin blindfold over his eyes and yanked him up and forward by the rope around his neck.

.   .   .

The blindfold was jerked off.

"Allow me, Lieutenant, to welcome you formally to the Imperial Nation of Japan and to Camp Sengei 4."

Watson heard the words, but mostly he saw two eyes. Dark brown eyes, larger and rounder than those in the other Japs he had seen so far. They came at him like twin spotlight beams. They were in the shaved head of a little Japanese man wearing an army officer's starched uniform with a shiny silver sword strapped on his waist. He appeared to be not much older than Watson—twenty or twenty-one at the most.

"I can surmise from your appearance and your odors that you have had a difficult time since your arrival in our glorious land, the Land of the Rising Sun. I believe the American word to describe your condition at this moment is *lousy*. You look and you are lousy, Lieutenant.

"I apologize for any rough treatment you may have received at the hands of our citizens," he said, his English only faintly accented. Watson could hardly believe it. If he closed his eyes, he could have been listening to somebody in Connecticut or New York. "But you must understand you are seen by the Japanese patriot as the ultimate devil, the most evil of all forces arrayed against our homeland in this war."

In his two hands he held a two-foot-long bamboo stick down across his body just below the belt. His feet, covered in highly polished brown boots that went to the knees, were slightly apart.

Watson was sitting in a chair four feet or so directly in front of him. Somebody had untied the rope that had held his hands together behind his back. But the rope around his neck remained in place.

"You and the other airmen of the United States Army Air Forces who fly the big B-29 bombers are murdering their grandmothers and grandfathers, their mothers and fathers, their children and their wives. You are setting them and their cities on fire with your bombs and burning their temples and their homes and schools and their bodies and souls to ashes. You are the ultimate white plague of all of our history, Lieutenant."

He walked forward and leaned his face down into Watson's. An awful smell of dead fish came flowing out of his mouth. "Do you understand that the average Japanese does not understand the evil that can motivate and stimulate and inspire you and your fellow Americans to swoop down out of our beautiful Japanese nights and spray fire and death on them?"

It was clearly not a question he wanted answered. His eyes were opened wide and lit up like neon. Watson tried to look away, but the man moved his face with Watson's. There was no escaping the rays of hate any more than the words or breath.

"Officially under the laws of Japan, you are a war criminal, Lieutenant. We have designated you and your kind 'special prisoners.' This camp is only for your kind. I am authorized to execute you at will at any time and in any fashion I wish. I am also authorized to keep you alive if it serves the interest of the emperor and of peace."

He stepped back and resumed his stance with the bamboo stick.

"I must add that another reason for any maltreatment of you may be that Japanese people also do not understand why you would allow yourself to become a prisoner, to be captured by the very people you are trying to destroy. Japanese people are taught about the honor of death over surrender. You Americans—*you,* an American officer—surrendered your honor in exchange for a dishonorable survival. They, the ordinary Japanese, have no respect for the surrenderers of this war because they themselves will never surrender no matter how many fires you ignite, how many cities you elimi-

nate, how many fields you scorch, how many bodies you cre-
mate, how many war crimes you commit."

Watson heard the words the man was saying, but he didn't
really hear the meaning. Watson felt as if both his body and
his mind were near death.

*Speak on, little Jap. I don't give a shit what you say be-
cause soon I will be dead — one way or another.*

He did speak, on and on.

"I, of course, clearly understand everything about you
Americans and what you have done and why you have done
it. I, too, am a combatant in this war. I, too, must commit
acts that in a more peaceful world and time I would not.

"I am an officer in the Imperial Army of Japan, and I, too,
hold the rank of lieutenant. I am a member of our superior
intelligence branch, the Kempei Tai. My special and privi-
leged duty for the emperor is as an interrogator, to speak directly to you surrenderers, you special-prisoner Americans
who fly down but do not fly back up and away. My mission
is to enlist your help in bringing this war to a rapid end so
more of your and our people will not die."

*Hold your breath, little Jap, while you wait for my help!
Hold your awful fishy breath!*

"You are fortunate to be in this camp, Lieutenant. There
are others for special prisoners that are in deep, dark dungeons where there are only rats and where the prisoners are
kept blindfolded and shackled and handcuffed around the
clock. We are lenient here. I have been given the authority to
use the techniques that I believe will be the most effective. I
know you Americans. You like to be treated nice. I will treat
you nice; you will be happy. No blindfolds, no hands tied.
So, you have, how you Americans say, won the roll of the
dice."

The little Jap officer used his bamboo stick to simulate a
roll of dice. It didn't quite work, but Watson got the point.

"I was chosen by the Kempei Tai for this very special and

important position by virtue of the fact that I speak your language as well as—if not better than—most Americans. Why, you might ask, does an officer in the Imperial Army of Japan stand here in front of you now speaking your language so well? The answer is one of birth and diligence. My father is a professor of literature who studied in your country as a young man and returned in his adulthood for four years to lecture and teach at the University of California at Berkeley. I was a small boy when he and my mother and my two sisters and I went to live in California; my parents insisted that I take the opportunity to learn the English language, and I did so. Upon our return to Japan, they insisted, too, that I maintain my English studies at an advanced level. It is a skill that has put me in this very special interrogator status in helping our army defend itself from the American racist onslaught."

The bright light dimmed slightly in the little Jap's eyes. A hint of a smile appeared at the edges of his mouth.

"Would you like something to drink, Lieutenant?" he asked.

"Yes, thank you," Watson said, speaking his first words since waking up tied to that wooden post immediately after he was captured. He had kept his mouth absolutely shut on the horrendous long ride in the back of the truck to this place, wherever it was, whatever it was exactly. He saw above and below the edges of the thin blindfold when they drove in that it was a grouping of several one-story wooden buildings enclosed by a tall barbed-wire fence; men who, at a glance, looked like other Americans were milling about outside.

The lieutenant-interrogator slapped his bamboo stick down on top of a small desk behind him. The *whack* brought a soldier into the room. He was told something in Japanese, and he left, returning shortly with a metal cup. After the soldier left the room, Watson expected the interrogator to hand him the cup. Instead, he placed it down on the desk.

"You must be very thirsty," he said.

"Yes, I am."

"Your bombing unit is based at Saipan, is that correct?" he asked, with no change of voice or inflection.

"I am not able to tell you that," Watson replied. "As you know, I am obligated under the Geneva convention to tell you only my name, rank, and serial number."

"As you also must know, the Imperial Army of Japan does not recognize the Geneva convention," he said calmly. "I already have that name-rank-serial number information from your metal identification tags, but now I need to know more about you, if I am to help my emperor end this war."

He leaned over Watson, who got another whiff of dead fish. His large eyes were now squinting, smaller. They resembled those of a small animal—a wildcat maybe?—and sent burning rays directly into Watson's own two eyes.

Watson said nothing and looked down. He could not hold the stare. It reminded him of playing stare-down when he was a kid. The first one to blink had to take out the trash.

"I take it your first and second names were drawn from your President John Quincy Adams? Is that correct?"

Watson said nothing.

"John Quincy Adams was the sixth president of the United States. Did you know that? *I* know that." Their faces were almost touching. The fish smell was unbearable. Watson tried to hold his breath.

The Jap officer said, "How many of your M-69 incendiary bombs were loaded on your plane last night when you left to set your fires of hell and destruction?"

Watson kept silent with his head down, breathing as best he could through his mouth.

"What is the name of your wing commander?"

"I cannot answer such questions," Watson said without looking up.

Watson heard him walk away. There were metal taps of some kind on the heels of his boots, and there was a loud *clap* on the wooden floor each time he took a step. Watson still didn't look up.

The steps came back toward Watson.

He suddenly felt a horrific pain on the top of his head, as if he had been whacked with a butcher knife. He glanced up to see the officer waving his bamboo stick like a baton. There was blood on it.

"Red blood on red hair," he said, as he clicked away. "There is symmetry in that, Lieutenant Fucky Duck John Quincy Watson." And he laughed. He laughed and laughed like a crazy man, a maniac, a hyena.

Watson was looking at him now to see if he was real. *Could this be a nightmare that will end with my waking up in the cockpit of* Big Red *on the runway at Saipan? If not, please,* please, *somebody kill me!*

John Quincy Watson closed his eyes and tried to think himself dead.

CHAPTER FIVE

Bishop Watson stared in disbelief at the man in the hotel room. He wondered silently, *How, dear Lord, could this fellow ever, ever see himself as a wonderful man?*

But he said to the man, "The word I used was *were*. I have no idea what you are like now. I am not going to hurt you, so don't be afraid. What happened was many years ago. Jesus died so that I can forgive."

"I did nothing that requires your forgiveness," said the elderly Japanese man. The voice, Watson now noticed, was much quieter and mellower than the Hyena's had been fifty years ago.

"We called you the Hyena," said Watson. "Did you know that?"

"You have confused me with somebody else."

"We called you that because of the way you laughed when you were beating and abusing us."

"I abused no one."

"Laugh for me."

"Get out of here right now."

"Please laugh for me. I want to see if you can still do it."

"Leave this room, sir, or I will call someone to remove you."

Watson shrugged and, with great labor and strain, got to

his feet and began an overdone crippled man's shuffle toward the hotel-room door. "I never knew your first name," he said. "The last name I knew like my own—Tashimoto. I think after the war that somebody said your first initial was *T*. What does the *T* stand for? What's your first name?"

"I have nothing to say to you about me."

Watson now stood right in front of the man. He moved closer, and they were less than a yard apart. He said, "Why do you deny who you are—what you did, what you were? I'm not here to hurt you. I saw you at the Dallas airport just now, and I traced you here. God meant me to see you at that airport and then find you here at this hotel. We must not deny God's will."

"God has nothing to do with what is happening here."

"He has something to do with everything in my life, Mr. Tashimoto. You don't deny that is your last name, do you? It is the one you used to register at this hotel."

"My name is Bill Joe Tashimoto. Please leave now."

"*Bill Joe* Tashimoto? Did you really say *Bill Joe*?"

It was obvious to Watson that this man felt he had just made a serious mistake. He clearly wished he hadn't told Watson that his name was Bill Joe. He turned away from Watson and walked, almost stiff-legged, to the door.

"How did you get a name like Bill Joe?" Watson asked.

The man said nothing, did nothing but put his hand on the doorknob as if waiting for Watson's departure.

"My first name is John," Watson said. "Middle name Quincy, as in the towns in Illinois and Massachusetts. John Quincy as in the fifth president of the United States—John Quincy Adams."

"Sixth," said Tashimoto.

"Sixth?"

"John Quincy Adams was the sixth president of the United States."

"I know that, and so did the Hyena know that. He—you—

told me that when you asked me my name during my first inter-rogation session. I said John Quincy and you said, 'Must be named for sixth president.' Caught you, Bill Joe. Why are you not able to admit who you are?"

"This conversation is over."

Watson, walking a bit faster and easier, went to the door, which Tashimoto quickly opened. Watson stopped and said, "I am a Methodist minister. I am, in fact, the retired Metho-dist bishop of San Antonio, Texas. Who are you?"

"I have nothing to say to you."

"With the Lord's help, I easily forgave you the permanent physical damage you inflicted on me. But I had much trouble forgiving you for what you got me to do to that Aussie. Do you remember that?"

"Out of here, please."

"Did you do that kind of thing so often that even that does not remain in your memory?"

Tashimoto reached up and slammed both hands against Watson's shoulders, attempting to push the bishop through the door and out into the hallway. Watson did not budge. He was a seventy-one-year-old man with a bad leg, but he was still six feet four inches tall and weighed 235 pounds. To an-other man of similar age who was five feet three and weighed about 130, John Quincy Watson was an immovable object.

"I will have you arrested!" Tashimoto screamed as he ran over to a telephone on the nearby writing desk.

Watson slammed the door closed and moved toward Tashimoto.

"Security, please," said Tashimoto into the phone. "I need to talk to someone."

Using his cane as a club, Watson knocked the phone out of the Japanese man's hand. He said, "Pick it up now and hang it up, please, Mr. Bill Joe Tashimoto."

Tashimoto did not move. "I will not do what you tell me to do."

"That's what I said to myself that day with the Aussie. You could not make me do what I didn't want to do," said Watson, picking up the phone and placing it back on the desk himself. He started to hang up the receiver when Tashimoto raised his right leg to kick.

Watson's reflexes were good enough to get that cane up there to deflect the kick short of its target, his groin.

"Not for a second time will you do that," Watson said. "Not for a second time will you practice your karate kicks on me."

Tashimoto slowly sat down on the floor and crossed his legs. He closed his eyes and lowered his head as if praying.

"To what God are you praying, sir?" Watson said. "And what are you praying *for*? Forgiveness, possibly? That is the primary province of Jesus."

Tashimoto said nothing, did nothing. He kept his head down, his hands clasped together in his lap.

Watson shuddered at the image of the Hyena seeking entrance to the kingdom of heaven. *Any* kingdom of anybody's heaven. After a minute or more of silence, he decided to do a little praying of his own. He closed his eyes and said out loud, as if from a pulpit to a church full of worshippers, "Our Heavenly Father, the Father of us all, help this poor man before me deliver himself from the sins of his past, from the crimes he has committed against me and others. Help him see that until he confesses, until he cleanses his conscience and makes peace within himself, his soul will rot, smolder, and eventually die in hell. Help him raise his head like a man, open his scary brown eyes and say the words of sorrow and redemption that will rid his soul and his very being of the crimes he committed against so many . . ."

Tashimoto raised his head and opened his eyes. Then he said, "You have the wrong man. Leave this room and leave me alone."

"You knew John Quincy Adams was the sixth president. The Hyena knew that. You just tried to kick me again the way you did before. Your eyes were burned into that part of my brain that contains the memory in such a way that there can be no mistake. You are the Hyena."

"I was not at that camp."

"Where were you then?"

"In Singapore."

"Doing what?"

"I was an interpreter for the Imperial Army of Japan."

"You are the Hyena."

"I am not!"

"You are!"

"No!"

"There can be no absolution for sin until you confess it and come to peace with it."

"I have nothing to confess!"

"I saw you personally kill several men!"

"You did not!"

"You called us flyers 'the white devils.' You said we were all war criminals who deserved to die because we were the ones who had flown bombing missions over Japan. You said we weren't like normal soldiers. You said white men with red hair like me were particular devils. You also said 'fucky duck' to us all the time. Say 'fucky duck.' Say it right now."

"I will never say such a foul thing."

Watson said, "You spoke perfect English except when you said 'fucky duck.' You said it with a pidgin kind of Japanese accent. Very funny, you were."

Tashimoto closed his eyes and bowed his head again. "You are speaking of matters that occurred fifty years ago," he said, keeping his head down. "You are the one with a need to come to a peace, Mr. Bishop."

"I have," Watson replied. "I have."

CHAPTER SIX

The Jap officer stopped his horrendous laughing. It startled Watson into opening his eyes.

He was still alive.

"My questions, again, Lieutenant, are: How many bombs were you carrying? What is the name of your wing commander? From what base did you fly?"

Watson shook his throbbing head. There would be no answers to those questions.

"Stand up!" the Jap shouted.

Watson stood up.

Suddenly, the Jap was right in front of Watson. His right foot left the ground, and before Watson could cover himself it landed right in the center of his groin. Watson had never felt anything so painful in his life. Not even the pole to the stomach or the hack to the head were close. It felt as if every cell, every nerve in his body had been bludgeoned, all at once, with a sledgehammer.

Watson grabbed himself and bent over. He must have screamed or yelled, but he didn't remember exactly what sound of suffering he made. The next thing he felt was another kick under the chin, which threw him backward down on the floor.

The awful little man laughed again for a while and then said, "I am an expert in the arts of self-defense we call karate and jujitsu, Lieutenant. But I must keep my skills finely tuned, because, like knowing the English language, they can disappear with disuse. People with red hair serve particularly well as drill-and-practice objects. You got it, fucky duck?"

Watson had hit the floor on the back of his head and was almost unconscious. He felt dizzy and frantic but aware that now, lying there on the floor, he was even more vulnerable to whatever this little shit had in mind.

Now as never before, not even when he was on the road with the first soldiers, Watson found himself hoping the next stage in this ghastly drama would be for a bullet to be put through his brain. *End this, little Jap, end this, please.*

But that wasn't what the little Jap had in mind. There were more questions—endless, pointless, mind-numbing questions that had nothing to do with anything important or classified.

The horrendous pain of the two kicks still reverberating through his body, Watson mouthed words about his elementary, secondary, and college educations and the town in Connecticut where he grew up. He murmured a few things on learning history and civics and English literature. Speaking as if on a kind of autopilot, he recited the Pledge of Allegiance and seven of the Ten Commandments, the teams in both the American and National leagues.

Then suddenly the Jap asked, "Do you have a wife, Lieutenant?"

"No."

"A mother?"

"Yes."

"A father?"

"Yes."

"Would you like for them to know that you survived your murderous mission and are alive as a prisoner of war of the Imperial Army of Japan?"

"Yes."

"Cooperate with me, Lieutenant Watson, and they shall be notified through proper channels. Do not cooperate and they will not be. They will think you are dead, which you probably will be before much more time passes if you do not cooperate. The choice is yours."

He asked the military questions again. Again Watson did not answer.

The Jap, furious, grabbed the rope leash that was still around Watson's neck and pulled up. Watson stood.

Again there was the kick to the crotch and then under the chin.

This time the kicks were not as wracking, the pain not as universal as the first time. The part of the brain that handles the transmission of pain must have been on shutdown, or the cells and nerves throughout his body were on overload—there had been a pain brownout, maybe?

Barely conscious, he heard heels on the floor and a door open. The Jap shouted something at somebody, and soon Watson felt two men on either side of him. Together, they lifted him up. He could tell by their size that they were not Japs.

The one on the left was tall and redheaded like Watson.

He whispered to Watson as they dragged him away, "These bastards are not going to get away with this. I promise."

.   .   .

They walked him down a hall, outside over a dirt path, and into another wooden hut. It was only after they lay Watson down in the middle of a floor crowded with other men that he had a chance to really look at his two escorts. They were Americans, and both appeared to be in worse shape than he was. They were filthy, thin, haggard, unshaven, bruised, torn, cut, miserable, angry.

They told him this place was a former copper mine called Sengei 4 that no longer had any copper or any other purpose than as a place to keep "special prisoners"—mostly American airmen who went down during bombing raids over Tokyo.

The redhead said he was Henry Howell, a B-29 pilot who had been at this camp ten weeks. The other identified himself as Jack Lederer, a B-29 navigator who had been captured and brought here eight days ago.

It was Henry Howell who gave Watson the worst of the bad news.

"What he—the Hyena—did to you just now is the very least of what will be done to you every day. There are no mines to work, no roads to build, no factories to run, no fields to plow, so fucking with us is their only activity. They are smelling defeat and their own deaths and disgrace. They hate us, the white devils, for whipping their holy yellow asses and most particularly for firebombing their cities, and they want to kill each of us one at a time. Some slowly, some quickly. Because you've got red hair like me, they'll use you for karate practice and other cute projects before leaving you for dead one day like you're a used sack of shit. I've lasted longer than most because I have decided to last. You'll have to make the same decision. For some it is a matter of will, not of might. You want to live, you live. You want to die, you die. These little Jap shits can make some of the life-and-death decisions for some of us, but we have some to make, too . . ."

And Watson heard no more because soon he was unconscious—knocked asleep by exhaustion, pain, and fear.

.   .   .

At daybreak, the dreadful truth of Henry's forecast was demonstrated. They were roused by kicks and screams from Japanese guards and ordered outside into a formation. Watson was unable to count heads, but he guessed there were more than fifty prisoners—maybe as many as seventy-five. Most were barely able to walk or stand.

In a few minutes the Hyena appeared with an older Japanese officer, each strutting in a fresh uniform. They marched to a position in front of the formation and faced the prisoners. The other man—Colonel Togata, the camp commander, Watson later learned—hollered out an order, and two soldiers came up with a large block of wood about the size of a tall wastebasket. They set it down in front of the two officers.

Then the Hyena called out, "Captain Lederer, Prisoner 382, front and center!"

Jack Lederer, who was down the line on the left from Watson, shuffled out toward the two Jap officers and the block of wood. It seemed to take forever for him to arrive. Henry Howell, who was standing next to Watson on the right, said in a loud whisper, "Good-bye, Jack. You're a hero. Be proud."

The two soldiers pushed Lederer down to his knees and forced his head across the top of the wooden block.

And then, in less time than it took to say die, the Hyena unsheathed his sword, raised it high over his head with two hands, and severed the head of Captain Jack Lederer, U.S. Army Air Forces, from his body.

Jack Lederer's head, his two blue eyes half open, hit the hard brown dirt and rolled slightly to one side.

Tears came rushing into Watson's eyes. He gagged. He had had no food or drink in hours, so there was nothing much to vomit. But he dry-heaved onto himself and the ground in front of him.

"Here comes the Hyena," Howell whispered. "Protect your balls, Watson!"

His reactions were too slow. Watson heard the laugh and

there he was. He felt a whack from the bamboo stick across the right leg and then the kick into his groin before he could get his hands down there.

"I will give you plenty of reasons to be sick, Lieutenant Fucky Duck, before *you* die," said the Hyena as Watson fell forward, face first.

He put a foot on the back of Watson's head and mashed his face down hard into the ground, smothering Watson's heaves.

.   .   .

They killed at least one prisoner almost every day. It seemed to be an unspoken quota of some kind that often had no direct relationship to anything the victim might have done to deserve death or any other punishment.

Not all were beheaded. Some were simply shot in the head while waiting in line for the latrine; others were bayoneted or beaten with wooden clubs or rifle butts to an agonizing death in front of the others.

The man specially chosen for a public death the day after Jack Lederer was a tall British officer, about whom Watson knew nothing. He was called out of formation to stand in front of a small wooden platform. The Hyena, too short to function otherwise, stepped up on the platform and, with a deftness that could only have come from a lot of practice, broke the Brit's neck. He did so by placing his right hand on the man's forehead, the left on the back of his neck, and then snapping them forward at the same time.

Watson thought he would always hear the *crack* sound.

The day after that it was a sergeant from Tulsa, Oklahoma, who had been a tail gunner on a B-29. The Hyena, with help from two soldiers, drowned the sergeant by holding his head down in a bucket of water until he stopped moving.

The sergeant had said nothing. None of them did. That silence from the dying struck Watson as odd. Why did people not scream to the heavens when they were about to die at the hands of these barbarians? Why did they not cry out in pain with the crack, the cut, the whack?

At first Watson woke up every day assuming this would be his day to go. Henry Howell did everything he could to encourage positive thinking, even teaching the vilest of things to call the Hyena in Latin. But it was almost hard not to volunteer, to go to the Hyena and say, What about choosing me today? I am ready to die. Kill me, oh noble Japanese *mentula fellator cunnus.*

The Japs did not count natural deaths as meeting the day's quota. So those who died from starvation, disease, or various injuries, or who simply chose not to wake up one morning were taken away and buried.

Some, in pain or otherwise unable to go on, committed a form of suicide. They didn't hang themselves or slit their wrists or lie down in front of trains. They did things so provocative the Japs had no choice but to kill them. There was a New Zealand pilot suffering from wet beriberi so bad his stomach was swollen as if he were pregnant with triplets and his testicles were like soccer balls. This man in pain simply started a silent, laborious walk from morning formation toward the front gate. The Japs yelled at him to stop—so did some of his fellow prisoners—but he only grinned, shot his right hand high in the sky, his middle finger up, and kept hobbling in the direction of freedom. Two guards quickly caught him and bayoneted him to the ground. The Hyena then ordered the New Zealander's bloated, bleeding, heaving body—he was still alive—brought back to the chopping block for a final rite of beheading. The Hyena did the deed himself with his sword. Watson got only a glimpse of the pilot's head there on the ground, but it looked like there was a smile on its face. He had gotten them to do his dirty work, to put him out of his misery. He controlled his passing—perhaps he saw that as something to smile about even as he died a most horrible death.

Watson was put on the burial detail, a task that came right out of every Sunday-school horror story of what life in hell would be like. He helped carry off dead men to some nearby woods, dug a hole, tossed them in, and covered them up. Once, while they were digging, the Hyena showed up unexpectedly and accused one of the team—a B-29 flight engineer from Kentucky—of not working hard enough. The Hyena stood over the kid while another hole was dug, and then he stabbed him through the heart with his sword, laughed his joyful howl, and ordered the rest of the detail to cover up the grave. The kid was not dead yet when they threw on the first spadefuls of dirt, but before long he was. Watson was able to smile and bow and call the Hyena—in an inaudible whisper—a *mentula fellator cunnus* to his face, but it did not mitigate the horror.

Another morning he went out with the burial detail after two days of torrential rain and found that seven or eight of the previously buried bodies had been washed up from their shallow graves. Some were partially decomposed into grotesque forms; others were covered with indescribable insects. Something had caused the brown eyes of one man to pop back open, and they were staring straight up at the sky as if in disbelief that some god had decided he would die and be buried in what was as close to hell on earth as the devil himself could have created.

The only positive thing about burial detail was that it brought Watson to conduct his first religious services. None of the others on the team had any interest in praying over the dead or doing anything other than finishing the awful job each day and getting out of there. Watson began reading aloud from a small copy of the New Testament one of the dead men had left behind and reciting his bedtime prayer for the Lord to please, *please* take this soul away. After the third or fourth day he began offering an original prayer for each dead man. Watson found these short services surprisingly comforting; they became the single part of his day that he viewed with anything close to pleasant anticipation. The only religious experience he brought to the task was his reluctant and occasional attendance at a Methodist Sunday school back in Westbrook.

His daily life was more awful than anything he could have imagined beforehand. The mild warnings from the intelligence briefer about what to expect as a prisoner of the Japanese were, innocently or intentionally, way short of the reality. It was just as well. Otherwise, everybody would have chosen to go down with their planes.

The Hyena's initial "roll of the dice" speech about Sengei 4 being better and easier than the other Kempei Tai places for special prisoners seemed ludicrous to Watson; nothing could be worse than this.

They were on starvation rations—a lump of rice the size of a golf ball every two or three days, some pigeon broth or other thin soup occasionally. The water tasted horrible and was contaminated, since sanitation was nonexistent. There was no medicine and no trained medical personnel. The prisoners slept on dirty grass mats thrown down on bare, badly splintered wooden floors, the distance between men being less than eighteen inches on both sides. There were no Red Cross packages; no cigarettes, no mail; no books or magazines; no razors, toothbrushes, soap, or toilet paper; no writing paper, no pens or pencils.

Every day, including what passed routinely and samely as Saturday and Sunday, Watson was interrogated for at least an hour. The questions were mostly the same—the military ones that Watson did not answer and the life-story ones he did. The Hyena did the questioning at the beginning, but eventually a sergeant the prisoners called Whiz Bang took over the duty. Whiz Bang spoke broken English and read the questions off a card. He paid no attention to the answers because he clearly did not understand them.

As Henry Howell had predicted, Watson's special hell was karate practice. He and Howell, the only redheaded prisoners, were taken two or three times a week to a room in that headquarters building where he first met the Hyena. The two of them were kicked, punched, tossed, slammed, and generally used the way rubber dummies might have been. Watson tried hard to protect his groin and private parts, but the Japs always found a way to trick him with a feint of some kind that left them exposed for a kick. After a while Watson grew bloodied and numb down there. He felt it but he didn't. Henry perfected a technique that Watson could not match. He defended himself by quickly bending his knees so he took the kicks and damage to his stomach rather than to what he referred to as "his future family's most valuable possessions."

The Hyena accompanied his karate chops and kicks with regular whacks of his bamboo stick on Watson's left ear and right calf. He did the same to others, but Watson's calf quickly got infected and the damage grew each day because there was no way to treat it except by wrapping it in strips of dirty cloth scavenged from the personal effects of dead prisoners.

Watson was ashamed then and remained ashamed at the way some of the prisoners fought over the shoes, shirts, underwear, and other belongings of their dead comrades.

There was one fight in particular that he would never forget. It was between two Americans over who was going to get a pair of flight boots that had belonged to the recently de-

ceased Jackson Wiley of Nebraska. The two prisoners beat
each other for nearly a half hour. It didn't end until one of
them had strangled the other to death with his bare hands.
Right there in front of all, one American killed another
American over a pair of boots!

A kind of resigned numbness kept the others from exert-
ing themselves enough to stop it. Watson despised his own
inaction. They buried the loser as just another death that had
been caused by their brutal captivity.

In other words, not all of the animals at Sengei 4 were
Japs.

.   .   .

Jackson Wiley had been one of three prisoners who had simply gone to sleep and not awakened. The other two were sick
or hurt. But Wiley had nothing wrong with him. He had been
a piano teacher and church music director in Nebraska before
being drafted into the army and made a radio operator on a
B-29. His own will was the specific weapon of death.

Watson said very little over Wiley's body when they
buried him because he could think of nothing to say that
wasn't scary.

Wiley's sleeping area was right next to Watson's, so they
had had an immediate opportunity—and need, really—to get
to know each other. But Wiley wasn't having any of that. He
barely talked and would seldom look at Watson when he
did. Nebraska and the music thing were about all Watson
ever found out about him. There were no conversations
about family, hopes, dreams, or much of anything else. Watson didn't even know Wiley's exact age, although he seemed
slightly older than the rest of them. Twenty-five or six
maybe. He was thin, but because he was also short—a good
seven or eight inches shorter than Watson—he didn't seem
malnourished or diseased. The scant rations seemed merely

to keep his body in its normal condition. Except for the way it shook, which it did most of the time. It seemed like a nervous condition, a form of palsy or something that kept his arms, hands, legs, cheeks, and eyelids in perpetual motion, even when he was asleep. Henry and others talked about his being sick, but there was no other symptom of illness. He seemed to always be at top physical strength when it came to walking, lifting, and other exertions. And his eyes didn't reveal illness around the edges of the whites. Watson finally concluded that Wiley was afraid. Every moment of every day he was afraid of what was going to happen to him.

Watson joined Henry in preaching to him steadily about thinking only about right now, only about the fact that he was alive right now. Don't think about the next minute or hour or day or week. One breath at a time, Jackson, they said over and over again. They also pleaded with him to remember and perform music in his head, to hear great performances or records. None of it seemed to register. Watson and the others knew he was headed for something terrible, but nobody knew what it would be.

One morning the din of wake-up began. There were shouts from the guards and then the prisoners. Everyone, as usual, was on his feet within seconds. Everyone except Jackson Wiley, who remained on his grass mat next to Watson's, fast asleep. Watson leaned down. "Hey, Jackson! Reveille!"

He didn't move. Then Watson noticed that the awful shaking was gone from Wiley's body. He reached down and grabbed Wiley by his head and then his shoulders. His eyes still didn't open. Henry kicked him on the bottom of his feet. There was no response. Watson was then hit by the smells of what had flowed out of his body. Jackson Wiley was a dead man. They turned him over and looked at him from top to bottom.

There wasn't a mark on him.

CHAPTER SEVEN

Watson retrieved his tiny electronic Rolodex from his left suit-coat pocket, found Henry's number, and dialed it.

The man who still referred to himself as the late Henry Howell—just as Watson called himself the late John Quincy Watson, because both lived through so many experiences they had entered believing they were as good as dead—answered the call on the first ring. It was almost ten o'clock on Martha's Vineyard, where he now lived most of the time.

"The Hyena is alive and well, and he's sitting here on the floor before me as I speak," said Watson.

"Can't be," said Howell matter-of-factly. "The son of a bitch is dead."

"That's what I thought, but here he is."

Watson told Howell about the eyes in the airport, the flight to San Diego, about tracking Tashimoto to this room on the eighteenth floor of this hotel overlooking beautiful San Diego Bay.

"What about the laugh?" Howell said. "I can still hear that goddamn laugh."

"I tried to get him to laugh, but he won't do it."

"The walk?" Howell said. "I'd know that walk from a hundred yards."

Watson had forgotten the walk. He looked down at Tashimoto and said, "Get up and walk around for a minute, please."

"Don't say please to that bastard!" Howell said. "Never say that to him—never!"

Tashimoto did not move. He remained sitting with his head down, hands folded in his lap.

Watson told Howell he was sure this was the Hyena, explaining about John Quincy Adams, the look and feel of the man, and again, mostly, the eyes.

"No man could have survived what we did to him," Howell said.

"No man except this one, apparently."

"Kill him again, Quincy," Howell said.

"What? Hey, Henry, I can't do that."

"They'll give you a medal."

"No!"

"Well, then, hold him however you've got him until I can get there. I'll do it."

"You can't be serious."

"Never more so, Right Reverend Bishop Watson."

"But you're a Right Honorable federal judge—"

"Retired. Double jeopardy applies here. We killed him once and paid the penalty, so this one is a freebie. No way we can be penalized a second time for the same crime."

"We weren't penalized in any way whatsoever the first time, and you know it."

"We paid a price in private guilt and shame. It's a free throw, Quincy. Kill him."

"Guilt and shame are the specialties of my line of work, Henry, not yours."

"Is that a slur against the law profession, Quincy?"

"Yes."

"It'll make for a great trial. The cameras and the Geraldos will come from miles around to make you another O.J. Step

right up, folks, to another trial of the century—the trial of
the late John Quincy Watson; a Methodist bishop—"

"Retired."

". . . murders—in a crime of wild, passionate, and justified
retribution—a subhuman Jap war criminal known as the
Hyena.

"The least you can and must do is make him understand
what it was like. Give him a little of his own medicine,
Quincy. Whack on him, kick him, torture him. Do unto him
as he did unto us and many, many more like us. Remember
what he did to Jack Lederer? Whacked his head off and then
laughed like a hyena?"

Watson remembered that. Of course, he remembered that.
For the first months in the hospital in San Antonio after the
war that memory was among those that kept Watson from
sleeping and doing other things that normal human beings
did.

"Remember Roosevelt night, Quincy? And what about
the Korean cook? You remember that?"

Watson remembered. But he had moved on, he had forgiven, he was at peace.

"How much of your red hair do you have left today?"
Howell asked. "It's been a while since I saw you."

"I'm down to one or two vague and ambiguous strands.
You?"

"A couple of my pubic hairs still look red if you stand
back several yards and squint."

Watson said to Howell, "I'll call you back."

"When?"

"In an hour or so."

"You can do plenty of damage to that little son of a bitch
in an hour or so, Quincy. Have you got your cane?"

"Always."

"Think of it as a piece of bamboo."

Watson watched as Tashimoto uncoupled his hands, raised his head, and looked up at him.

"In an hour or so," Watson said to Howell and hung up the phone.

CHAPTER EIGHT

Roosevelt night.

They were awakened by the sound of festive, happy Japanese music playing over the camp's seldom-used public-address system. Within minutes, several guards, half-dressed and guzzling sake, burst into the hut shouting, "Roosevelt dead! Roosevelt dead!"

They turned on the lights and ordered the prisoners to their feet.

And in behind the guards strutted the Hyena, as if he were a little boy king arriving at his own birthday party. He was dressed only in an undershirt, his uniform pants, and boots, and he was grinning and gesturing with his sword high over his head.

"Your war-criminal president is dead!" he screamed. "Our brave soldiers have killed him! The war is all but over!"

The prisoners stood silent.

It had never occurred to Watson that Franklin Delano Roosevelt would die. FDR was not a popular political figure among Watson's father and his Republican friends in Connecticut, but, my God, he was the president! He was our commander in chief of this war! How could the Japs have gotten close enough to kill him?

The Hyena, clearly as full of booze as some of his troops, pranced down the rows of prisoners, screaming, "You war-criminal swine will now shout the American way: 'Roose-velt's dead! Hip, hip, hooray!' "

None of the fifty-three prisoners uttered a word.

"I repeat. All together now, on three—one . . . two . . . three: 'Roosevelt is dead! Hip, hip, hooray!' "

The Hyena stopped in front of Jerry Lipscomb of Ana-heim, California. He was a P-51 fighter pilot who had been shot down while flying escort for a B-29 sortie over an im-portant Japanese water route known as the Shimonoseki Strait. Watson didn't much like Lipscomb because he was too arrogant and slick by half. Watson didn't know if it went with being a fighter pilot or being from California, or both.

The Hyena, cackling hysterically, brought the point of his sword to Lipscomb's navel. Lipscomb was wearing a filthy khaki shirt, so the spot was only an estimate . . . Then he pushed the sword forward—only slightly, about a quarter of an inch. Watson, who was standing diagonally across from Lipscomb, saw blood on both sides of the sword point.

Lipscomb said nothing, did nothing, and Watson's opin-ion of the man from California changed forever. This was one tough son of a bitch.

The Hyena pushed the sword in farther—another quarter inch or so. Lipscomb still showed no sign anything was hap-pening. More blood appeared on the sword blade.

Then Henry Howell yelled, "Let's hear it! Roosevelt's dead! Hip, hip, hooray! Roosevelt's dead! Hip, hip, hooray!"

Watson, without thinking, yelled, "Roosevelt's dead! Hip, hip, hooray!"

Three others joined in, followed by several more the next

time, and the next. Soon the hut was full of American, British, and Australian voices yelling over and over in unison, "Roosevelt's dead! Hip, hip, hooray! Roosevelt's dead! Hip, hip, hooray!"

The Hyena removed the sword from Lipscomb's stomach. Then he wiped the blood off on Lipscomb's shirt.

Lipscomb remained perfectly still—and quiet. He was the only one, to Watson's eye, who had yet to scream, "Roosevelt's dead! Hip, hip hooray!"

The choral shouting stopped, and the Hyena said, "And what do you say about the death of the evil American president, Lieutenant Lipscomb?"

Watson literally held his breath. Here now was this crazy fighter pilot from California making a life-or-death decision. Yell or die. The choice was his.

Lipscomb moved his eyes. Only his eyes. He did so in the direction of Henry Howell, who was standing next to Watson and, like him, was tall enough to be seen across the head of the Hyena.

The fighter pilot must have seen *Do it! It's not worth dying over!* in Henry Howell's face because Lipscomb then said in a flat, unemotional voice, "Roosevelt's dead. Hip, hip, hooray."

"Can you not speak louder?" asked the Hyena.

"Roosevelt's dead! Hip, hip, hooray!" shouted Lipscomb.

Watson was still afraid for Lipscomb. The Hyena, drunk as well as crazy and angry and cruel, might still plunge that sword through Lipscomb's middle. The little shit seemed capable of any inhumanity.

"Very well," said the Hyena after a few more seconds. He strutted away from Lipscomb. At the door he stopped and twirled around. "You Americans should know that a man named Harry Truman has taken over as president of your defeated nation," he said. "He is a shirt salesman from Kansas. He is a joke, and so are all of you."

And then he was gone.

After a while, in the dark, Watson and the others spoke among themselves. Could Roosevelt really be dead? Truman? Who in the hell was he besides the vice president? What in the hell does he know about winning a war or anything else?

Somebody said Roosevelt had been sick. The Japs didn't kill him. No way. He had polio or something when he was a kid. And then there was a heart problem. Somebody else said Truman was from Kansas City, Missouri, not Kansas. He once worked in a haberdashery there. And later went into politics as a member of a political gang—something like that. He wasn't a crook, but all the others mostly were. But he was a senator when FDR picked him for the ticket. And wasn't Truman in the army in World War I? The artillery maybe . . .

When Watson finally went back to sleep sometime later, he was in a fearful state of gloom and despair. The Hyena was right about one thing: The war was all but over. There was just no way the United States could win this war with Harry Truman as president, whoever and whatever he was.

·   ·   ·

The Korean cook.

Henry Howell of Birmingham, Massachusetts, was not only Jerry Lipscomb's leader, he was everybody's. Although at twenty-four he was only four years older than Watson and considerably younger than some of the others, he was their inspirer, prince, manager, coach. He was Watson's size—six feet four—so his physical presence was part of it, but he was also a man who reeked of smarts, confidence, and courage. It helped, too, that he had the rank of captain and had had more combat experience, having flown twenty missions in Europe with B-17s before being sent to the 20th Air Force to fly B-29s. He and Watson had never met before because

Howell's wing flew from Tinian, the other island in the
Marianas that the army and marines had taken from the
Japanese for use as B-29 bases.

Howell made it his mission at Camp Sengei 4 to help
everyone stay in the fight. He worked on their heads, their
state of mind. First, he kept the prisoners agitated, alert, and
eager, and unforgiving of their captors. In the daytime he ran
quiet, ongoing discussions on revenge, on how they would
make these little Jap bastards pay for what they were doing
to them. At night he ordered them to be peaceful and at ease,
urging them to dream about good things—great baseball
catches or hits they had witnessed or executed, dramatic
football games played or watched, beautiful sunsets seen,
marvelous books read, swims or hikes or runs taken, new
Chevys and Fords and Caddies driven or longed for, beautiful movie stars—Hedy Lamar and Lana Turner, particularly—lusted after.

Watson had trouble at first conjuring pleasant dreams.
Every time he closed his eyes at night he was back in *Big Red*
with smoke and heat and death shooting up on him from below. He couldn't stop himself from picturing in vivid color
those final moments in the cockpit before he yelled, "Bail
out!"

When he did finally manage to move on to something
nice, he envisioned a great moment in the athletic sun as a
freshman forward on the Amherst basketball team. They
were trailing Wesleyan by one point with only two seconds
remaining on the clock. One of the guards threw the ball to
Watson and yelled, "Shoot!" Watson was thirty-five feet
from the basket, but he jumped and pushed off the ball as
hard as he could. The ball zipped through the net without
touching the rim just as the final buzzer was sounding. *We
won the game and I was the hero:* Watson must have said
that to himself hundreds of times as he lay on his filthy pad
on the floor in that terrible little building in that horrid place

called Sengei 4. The scene was a complete fabrication, of course. The closest he had ever come to being a basketball hero was in their second game against Williams, which Amherst won by four points; Watson scored twenty-one of his team's fifty-six points.

The survival technique Watson admired—and envied—the most was the one Fred Hitt from South Carolina perfected. He did in his head what Wiley was either unable or unwilling to do with music. Hitt went back to school in his mind, beginning with his very first day in the first grade. Every day, he woke up and vividly imagined getting ready to hop the bus that took him to St. John's Elementary in north Charleston. Once there, he talked with his friends until the first bell and then went to homeroom for show-and-tell. Then there was spelling drill and arithmetic and art and music. On and on, Monday through Friday, week after week, he re-created in his mind in real time each lesson, each drill, everything that had happened. At any given moment in their awful day as prisoners of the Japanese, one could ask Hitt: Where are *you* right now? "I'm at the blackboard doing multiplication tables," he'd say.

There was more to Henry's survival approach than sweet memories and dreams and bad talk. He believed they either remained in the fight or they died. And if dying was what they wanted to do, then why in hell did they go to the trouble of jumping out of airplanes and screwing around with parachutes and everything else each of them in their own way did to survive?

Fighters survive to fight, Henry told them.

He decided the best way of remaining in the fight was to cause as many problems as possible for the Hyena and his little band of nasty Japs. But it had to be done in ways that did not trigger retribution or make their terrible situation any worse than it already was.

That pretty much eliminated acts of violence against Jap

guards, stealing food or supplies, or doing anything major and obvious. There were also cultural differences to be considered. Watson and the others figured it would have been easy, for instance, to have made their primitive plumbing and cooking systems inoperative, but they concluded the nasty little Japs would barely have noticed or cared. To the prisoners' sour—and yes, racist—observation, they seemed to have the hygiene habits of cats and rats, the eating habits of pigeons and squirrels. The task was to come up with something fresh every day that was annoying enough to give the prisoners pleasure but small enough not to get any of them killed or otherwise punished.

They discovered that Japs were afraid of mice. So they worked hard at capturing mice live and then, instead of eating them in accordance with accepted survival instincts, setting them free at specially chosen moments to cause the most havoc. The happiest day was when a guard called Drip ran away from a mouse, kept running through the front gate, and disappeared. The Hyena sent a search party out to find him, but as far as was known, they never did. The nightly joke was to guess how far away from Sengei 4 Drip was tonight. Halfway to California? Honolulu? Australia?

Japs, the prisoners were told, had weak night vision. And they hated owls. So owl sounds were made in the middle of the night, triggering wild chasing around in the dark as Japs tried to find them. They were told Japs lived in constant fear of evil spirits. One of the Aussies was a fluent writer of Japanese, so he wrote up warnings from spirits on trees and the ground and on scraps of paper that were left lying around.

The major achievement was the theft of the wooden block that was used in beheading. Under the cover of darkness a group of prisoners took it to the shed where the corpses were kept for burial. The next morning Watson and the burial detail buried the block in a grave with one of their dead colleagues. The burial-detail guards were particularly stupid and lazy as well as interested in staying as far away as possible from the blood and the stench, the maggots and the other sheer awfulness that went with handling corpses. They were easy to deceive. Watson figured they could have buried a truck or a B-29 and the guards wouldn't have seen it.

The most effective steady weapon was to start rumors among the Japs, originating most of them through one particular burial-detail guard. To put it charitably, he was the single dumbest Jap soldier ever to come to their attention. He was called Grunt Grunt to commemorate the only two sounds anyone ever heard him make.

One morning, under his watchful eye, Watson made a big thing of picking up a lone blackberry that he pretended to have found on the pathway to the burial area. Berries grew plentiful and wild around the camp, but the prisoners were never allowed to pick any for themselves. They were reserved for the Hyena and his chosen favored ones.

Watson popped the berry in his mouth, then, as Grunt Grunt moved to mete out punishment, doubled over as if in agonizing pain and fell flat on his face and—to a dumb Jap soldier—unconscious. Within an hour all of the berries in the camp commissary and on the vines were burned because they were thought to be poison.

Through Grunt Grunt and others, rumors were started about the suicide of Tōjō, cholera epidemics, impending Chinese commando raids, and truckloads of comfort girls on their way from Korea. It was the ultimate of pleasures to observe the Hyena's crew coping with each imagined crisis. The only off-limits rumor subject was Emperor Hirohito because, according to scuttlebutt picked up by one prisoner, even the mention of the emperor's name by an American prisoner could mean instant death.

There was only one serious mistake. And it was truly tragic.

Howell and a Brit somehow got a guard at the latrine, the apparent second-dumbest Jap soldier on earth, to believe that the main Korean cook in camp was an American spy who was slipping military secrets out to MacArthur and Eisenhower. Word finally reached the Hyena, who ordered the cook boiled to death in a huge soup vat. They made the prisoners watch. The poor man tried desperately to climb out of the vat. Each time he was beaten back by a soldier's rifle butt until he didn't try again.

Henry Howell was as mortified as any at the horror he and the Brit had set in motion. But he said, "We didn't put the guy in the soup. Remember that—the Japs killed him, not us. We did not put him in the soup. Got it? Our hands and consciences are clean."

The sound and smell of that Korean man lingered with Watson for several days and caused him and the others to cease small combats against the Japs—but only for a while. The fight to survive had to go on.

CHAPTER NINE

"I am going to use the bathroom," said Tashimoto as he uncrossed his legs and stood up.

Watson said, "You called it the *benjo* at Sengei 4—we all did. And you just went a few minutes ago because I heard the toilet flushing. I hope you don't have an internal medical problem. It took almost three years for my pipes and canals and various other internal things to operate correctly after my time with you."

Tashimoto said nothing and started for the bathroom door. Watson moved as fast as he could behind him and threw his cane up between the doorjamb and the door to keep Tashimoto from closing the door fully behind him.

"The telephone," Watson said. "Disconnect the receiver from the cord and hand it to me, please."

"I will not," said Tashimoto. "This is as silly and childish as it is criminal."

With a sudden lunge, Watson put all of his weight against the door. The little Japanese man on the other side was unable to stop the force of the big American. The door flew open and Watson lost his balance. As he reached for a door-knob or something to break a potential fall, Tashimoto raised his right hand in a karate move and lashed it toward Watson's left arm.

The blow landed on Watson's biceps. He winced, smiled, and then, using his right arm, whipped the cane through the air over his head. Tashimoto stepped back.

"Henry said I should think of this as a piece of bamboo," Watson said. "Relax; I'm not going to use it on you." Tashimoto sat down on the closed commode seat. He did not look at Watson. "Do you remember Henry Howell?" Watson continued. "His number was 369B. He was tall, too, like me. He also had red hair. You must remember him from his accent, if nothing else—heavy Massachusetts. You know Henry. You kicked him in the stomach. Time after time, you kicked him in the stomach."

Tashimoto shook his head twice but said nothing.

"Henry Howell was the one who knew Latin and kept telling you what a fool and a criminal and an ass and a swine and a murderer you were in Latin. He said terrible, vile things about you that you never understood. Neither did most of the rest of us, but it helped us to know he was saying them. You remember him? You must! It will really hurt his feelings if you don't."

"I remember no one," Tashimoto said, still not looking at Watson.

Watson reached across to the wall and grabbed the telephone receiver. He easily pinched it off from the coiled cord. "Remember the old-style telephone system?" he said. "It took a repairman, an appointment, and seven days to get a headset fixed, attached, or removed. Now we can do it ourselves just like that . . ." He almost laughed out loud at what he had just said to this little man on the commode. It was ridiculous to think the Hyena would know about life with telephones before Ma Bell was broken up in the name of progress, competition, and other good American Way things.

Still holding the phone receiver, Watson turned to leave, then remembered something else. He reached for the roll of toilet paper next to the commode. "I ought to take this so you can try it without paper the way you made us," he said. "Remember the time you made that kid from somewhere in the Midwest wipe himself with a piece of tree bark? You were upset because he walked too slowly to a formation. You made him do it over and over in front of all of us until he was bleeding."

Watson then left Tashimoto to his privacy in the bathroom and walked back out to the sitting room and over to the large sliding glass door that looked out onto the bay. He opened the door and stepped onto the small balcony, which was furnished with an outdoor table and three chairs. The sky was lit up by the bluish orange of a setting sun; the air was fresh and cool. It was a most pleasant evening here in San Diego.

A large gray navy ship was docked across the bay at what looked like a navy base of some kind. Twenty or thirty small sailboats and yachts moved in all directions. Directly in front of the hotel was an outdoor restaurant, a huge swimming pool, and an elaborate patio, flanked by a yacht basin.

He turned back around in time to see Tashimoto come running out of the bathroom. At first Watson thought he was racing toward the front door, but he headed straight to the balcony and Watson.

Again Watson used the cane as he had on the bathroom door. He stuck it out just in time to keep the door from closing and thus trapping him outside on the balcony.

Now Tashimoto made a run for the front door. There was no way Watson could catch him. End of my strange little World War II reunion, he thought.

But before he got to the door, something caused Tashimoto to trip and fall facedown, spread-eagled on the floor.

Watson moved as swiftly as he could to a position between the downed man and the door. "A higher power is in charge of both of us, Mr. Tashimoto," he said. "That power brought us together and continues to keep us together." Tashimoto lifted his head. Watson saw some blood around the bottom of the little man's nose. "I hope you didn't hurt yourself. Are you all right?"

Tashimoto closed his eyes and put his head back down on the marble entranceway floor.

Watson, without thinking, slapped his cane against his right pant leg. He was struck—frightened, really—by how similar the sound was to the whack of a bamboo stick against the body of a human being.

"Talk to me!" he bellowed to the man on the floor.

"I have no desire to talk to you," said Tashimoto.

Watson whacked the cane hard on the sideboard in the entranceway. The sound was not unlike that of pistol shot. It startled Watson. The old noises kept coming back. This time Tashimoto's whole body visibly blanched. And soon he got himself up onto his feet and into one of the chairs by the sliding glass door.

Watson laid the cane across his lap and sat down in the other chair, directly across from him. Easy does it now, Watson said to himself. Calm down.

"Where do you live, Mr. Tashimoto?" Watson asked.

"In Tokyo."

"What are you doing here?"

"I am on a business trip."

"What do you do for a living, Mr. Tashimoto?"

"I am a vice president of the First Nippon Bank of Tokyo."

"What exactly do you do?"

"I explore investment-and-loan opportunities."

"What kind?"

"My specialty is the American business and industrial community."

"Do your employers and customers know you abused and killed American prisoners of war in World War II?"

Tashimoto said nothing.

"Is your work fun?" Watson continued.

"Fun is not the purpose of work."

"What *is* the purpose?"

"Please, please. I cannot have a conversation with you about matters like this."

Watson leaned down and raised his right pant leg up to the knee. "How about talking about this, then?" he said. His calf was half the normal size and covered with ugly red scar tissue.

"The army doctors told me fifty years ago that I should replace this awful thing with something artificial. They told me I would be a cripple and hurt every day forever if I didn't. They were right. I have been a cripple and I have hurt a little bit every day for almost fifty years."

Tashimoto glanced at Watson's leg and then looked out toward the sunset and San Diego Bay.

Watson went on. "I have had my second thoughts. Having an ugly, shriveled, scarred leg has meant never wearing shorts or swimming trunks in public. On several occasions, particularly on our regular beach trips to Corpus Christi and Padre Island—I live in Texas—I wished I had opted for the phony leg and gotten rid of that mess you created down there."

Tashimoto looked back toward Watson. "My little sister and my mother had worse scars—much worse scars—all over their bodies when they died," he said. "They were from burns from bombs dropped by American planes on our city."

"You think I killed your sister and mother?"

"I do not know what you did; I do not know who you are."

"Do you have children?" Watson asked.

"Yes, I do," Tashimoto answered. "Two boys and a girl."

"I have no children, and you know why, don't you?"

Tashimoto moved his head closer to Watson's. "I know nothing about you!"

"Those eyes give you away, Tashimoto. You can never hide your eyes; you can never escape being the Hyena."

Watson took the cane firmly in his right hand and raised it high above his head. "Do you remember the first time we met? You raised your bamboo stick like this and cracked it down across the top of my head so hard it drew blood. You thought that was hilarious, and you laughed and laughed. You must remember that?"

"If you are going to strike me, do so," said Tashimoto, moving his head to a position that made it an even easier target.

Watson lowered the cane back to his lap and said, "I do not strike people."

"Then this meeting is over and I would again ask that you leave," said Tashimoto. He started to stand but was settled back down in the chair by Watson's cane lowered gently onto his right shoulder.

"Explain the red-hair thing," Watson said. "I never understood it then, and I still don't."

"The redder the hair, the whiter the skin," Tashimoto said. Then he grabbed the cane with his left hand, jerked and twisted it away from Watson. He stood up with the cane raised above his head in both hands as if it were a sword.

CHAPTER TEN

An abrupt hush fell on Camp Sengei 4 one afternoon in August. It was as if God in heaven had tossed a giant army blanket down over that tiny, miserable part of the world. Suddenly, there seemed to be no sounds from wind, trees, birds, or people. The Jap guards moved in slow motion, speaking only in muffled voices and whispers to each other and eying their captives with silent grimaces and fearful stares.

Something important had happened, but the prisoners had no idea what it was.

They found out that night. One of the Jap supply sergeants told a British lieutenant assigned to mess and garbage duty that the Americans had dropped "a biggest bomb ever in world" on the Japanese city of Hiroshima. He said it supposedly came like a bursting thundercloud of fire and turned the city and its thousands of people into dust.

Could it be true? Watson and the others whispered fearfully among themselves about that possibility. What kind of bomb would it have been? Some of those who had been based at Tinian most recently said there had been talk of a special B-29 unit that would someday drop a magic atomic type of bomb on Japan, but that had been mostly dismissed as hopeful rumor.

They went to formation the next morning not knowing what to expect. Colonel Togata was not there. Only the Hyena. He seemed his usual angry self, only more so. But to their relief and surprise, he didn't kill anybody and the prisoners were quickly dismissed to go about a pointless day of complete idleness. There was only one prisoner to bury, a flight engineer from Ohio who had never been able to shake a horrendous cough, cause unknown. Two nights before he had coughed up so much blood that he bled to death.

The stillness continued for the next three days; then a guard reported to one of the prisoners that another of the catastrophic cloud bombs had exploded over the Japanese city of Nagasaki. Again, all living things were extinguished, all structures were incinerated.

God bless you, Harry Truman, whoever and whatever you are!

That night the quiet in the world of Camp Sengei 4 ended. The Hyena and a few of his soldiers forced Watson, Howell, and five others into his karate-practice room and announced at the top of his lungs that he was going to kill them all, one at a time, unless they told him, the official representative of the emperor of Japan, everything they knew about the new evil bomb from hell. You seven were selected, he said, because you were B-29 command pilots and thus had to know something.

Howell tried to head it off with some common sense, attempting to explain that any such bomb project would be so top-secret that only the president of the United States, Winston Churchill, and a handful of scientists and generals would know anything about it.

"You lying fucky duck!" the Hyena screamed as he gave Henry a quick kick in the stomach.

He kicked each of them several times. He also whacked with his bamboo stick and pricked with his sword and a bolo knife. The ferocity of his frustration was beyond even his normal bounds of anger. He shook and spit, sweated and snarled like a man on the verge of literally exploding into little pieces.

He chose Mack Ridley to kill first, slashing his stomach open with the knife. Ridley was short and stubby and from somewhere in Wisconsin. He was one of the last two B-29 pilots to join the prisoner ranks, having been captured ten days earlier by a Japanese patrol boat after bailing out over the Sea of Japan.

Ridley screamed to the heavens and beyond before he died there on the dirty floor of that room, blood pouring out of him.

"All right, all right," said Dick Larson, the other of the two American pilots taken that day, to the Hyena. "I'll tell you what you want to know."

Watson was stunned. Larson, as well as Ridley, had repeatedly and with conviction told his comrades that he knew nothing about any atomic bombs. Watson was also appalled that he was now considering telling the Japs about it or anything else.

Henry Howell, their leader, said firmly to Larson, "Tell them nothing, Larson. That's an order."

A Jap soldier knocked Henry out cold with the butt of a rifle. Watson thought Henry was a goner. But before the soldier could use his bayonet or fire a shot at Henry's fallen body the Hyena screeched at Larson, "Speak!"

Larson was probably at least nineteen, but he looked twelve. His blond hair was in a crew cut; his skin was white and fresh. His five feet eleven or so body was of modest build but still firm because he hadn't been on prisoner rations long enough to begin deteriorating.

He said to the Hyena, "Well, I never saw one of the bombs myself with my own eyes, but I understand they are about the size of an oil drum. They're made of a type of fission material that causes atoms to collide and that leads to a radioactive explosion more powerful than ten thousand regular bombs—"

"How many do you Americans have?" demanded the Hyena.

"Hundreds—maybe thousands. Enough to destroy the whole world, they told me."

"Are they going to drop a third one on Japan?"

"Yes."

"Where?"

"Kyoto."

The Hyena closed his eyes and, it seemed, his whole body. His arms went limp, and he bowed his head and then slowly dropped to his knees. "My Kyoto," he said. "My lovely Kyoto." Then he began to sob, to shake, to crumble onto the floor.

His soldiers, clearly confused and afraid, backed away and disappeared, leaving the American pilots in the room with this grieving maniac.

Without a word, the Americans moved. Watson and another helped Henry Howell to his feet. He was almost fully conscious now. Two others grabbed the still-bleeding corpse of Mack Ridley by the hands and feet. Larson, who had Ridley's two hands, threw up on himself and on Ridley's face. Nobody said anything or gave a sign of having even noticed.

Outside, they walked as quickly and quietly as they could. They went first to the corpse shed, where they laid out Ridley.

There were Jap soldiers around, but they seemed to not see—or care.

The seven Americans headed for their barracks.

"Well done, Larson," Henry said quietly.

"What?" Watson said. "He gave away military secrets—he's a goddamn traitor."

"Relax, Quincy," said Henry. "The whole thing was a setup."

"Yeah, I made it all up," Larson said. "I know nothing about any bomb."

"You made up Kyoto, too?"

"You bet."

"Why?"

"Why not?" said Henry, taking the responsibility. "Maybe they would believe Larson and let us live—we had nothing to lose."

"So your order to shut up was phony?" somebody else asked Henry.

"You got it," Henry said.

"You might have gotten killed," Watson said.

Henry waved that comment away. "I just wish I had thought of doing something like this before. There's a damned good possibility that the Hyena might pass it on to his fellow criminals higher up, who might get scared enough to end this crazy war."

. . .

It was the night of the leaflets that they decided to kill the Hyena.

They had not been told that the war was over, but they began to sense it when a few more days went by without any fresh prisoners being brought in. Up till the news of Hiroshima and Nagasaki, captured B-29 crew members had trickled in regularly at a rate of four or five a week.

They figured the Japs, down to their last angry days, were now immediately killing rather than capturing all white-devil Americans who fell from the sky. There seemed no other reason, because the flashing lights off on the horizon said that no matter what the big bombs had done, the B-29s and incendiary bombs were still coming night after night.

They knew they had really won the war when one of the young enlisted Jap guards was suddenly and absurdly friendly and nice. He gave each prisoner as much rice as he wanted, smiled while he did so, and did not hit any with the butt of his rifle as he had done to at least three of them every day until then. A few days later several of the most brutal guards disappeared.

Then a U.S. plane—a magnificent B-29, in fact—flew low over Sengei 4 dropping leaflets that told the Japanese soldiers that their emperor had surrendered unconditionally and that they should remain in place and be peaceful. They were warned of war-crimes prosecution if they in any way harmed or abused any of the prisoners under their control.

The leaflets told the prisoners to remain in place and be patient—help and freedom were on the way.

It made simple logical sense that the Hyena would soon have all of the prisoners killed—he might even do it single-handedly—before running for cover. Howell was the first to say they had to kill the little shit. We simply have to, he said. Watson agreed. They took no votes as such, but by Quaker consensus, as one of the guys who had gone to a Friends high school described it, it was decided that it was in their immediate self-interest as well as their patriotic and moral duty to make sure the Hyena was punished for his war crimes against all of those who died at Sengei 4.

Way before daybreak the next morning, twelve of them walked as a group out of the barracks to the Hyena's room in the headquarters building down the hall from where he practiced karate on Watson and Howell. There were a few Japanese soldiers around. They saw the prisoners, possibly even figured out what they were up to, but made no effort to stop them. The speeches the prisoners had heard about how differently the Japanese weighed honor over survival turned out to be less than accurate.

The need to survive beats in the souls of yellow heroes of the Rising Sun as well as white devils, thought Watson.

They stormed right into the Hyena's room, grabbed him from his bed in his underwear.

"You fucky duck bastards!" he yelled. "You will die for this!"

Five of them carried him by his arms and legs outside. He tried to kick and swat, but there were too many of them, too much force against him.

So he laughed his hyena laugh.

For once, it gave Watson pleasure to hear it. *Laugh and laugh and laugh, you little fucky duck bastard, all the way to your last breath!*

They took him to the corpse shed in the far corner of the camp compound, the place those on the burial detail went each morning to collect the day's dead. It was cramped with all of them inside, but it didn't matter. The Hyena had to die here.

There were three dead prisoners there that night. Watson knew two of them—a navigator from Florida and a copilot from New York City. Both had died of natural causes—if any death in Sengei 4 could be called natural. There had not been a beheading or any other public killing in several days. The third body belonged to someone Watson did not recognize. They were laid out naked next to one another. The skin of all three had turned gray, and their eyes seemed on the verge of popping out of their heads.

There had been a time when even looking at the sight of three dead men like this would have been an extraordinary event in Watson's life. Now he barely glanced at them. He saw them without really seeing them. Their smell, a horrific mixture of all that comes out of humans upon death, had become so commonplace it didn't really bother him that much either.

He had come to kill the Hyena. It was all he cared about that night.

Some of the others tried to get the Hyena to beg for mercy, but he refused to do so. He refused to say much of anything, in fact, other than "fucky duck," which he said over and over between cackles. The sound of that stupeifying laugh made it so much easier to do what they had come to do.

That was to slowly kick him to death.

They made a circle around him and then, one at a time, stepped over and kicked some part of his body. Watson did little damage. He could not use his right foot or leg, but he tried with his left foot, covered with the ragged remains of flying boots, to wham the little Jap shit in the groin. Time after time he stepped up and rammed his boot into him as hard as he could, which, given his diminished physical strength, wasn't very hard. He doubted that the Hyena felt any of his kicks. Some of the others were also having trouble landing really forceful hits. But nobody minded that much. It only meant that this miserable little creature would suffer longer before he died; and they were determined to make him suffer. Death was not enough of a punishment.

Henry Howell concentrated his kicks on the Hyena's stomach, because the little Jap had landed most of his karate shots at Henry's midsection. Others went at his face or the sides of his head. One or two moved around, determined to land a kick on every square inch of his small body.

Watson had become accustomed to the distinctive dull, soft, muffled sound of blows to the flesh and body. Just as the sights and smells of death had become routine in his life, so had the sounds. There are no other sounds like them.

"I die for the emperor," the Hyena said. He said it only once, in a barely audible voice that was weakening along with the rest of him. Then he moaned. But he never cried for himself as he had for Kyoto, never screamed in pain. He finally lost consciousness. They continued kicking for a long time after he closed his eyes and went limp. The pleasure never seemed to end.

When they finally left him he was nothing but bloody, mauled, bruised clumps of flesh.

CHAPTER ELEVEN

Watson hurt just from the thought of the crack that was about to come down on his once-red head. It was going to feel much like it did fifty years ago, only it would be administered by his own cane instead of a bamboo stick in the upraised hands of a little Japanese man.

"Once more from the beginning, fucky duck, I see," he said to Tashimoto.

It was all happening so fast there was no point in trying to move out of the way or even attempting to deflect the blow. So Watson closed his eyes and began to pray. He got as far as "Help me, Father, endure the pain and suffering that is about to befall me at the hands of this man. Help me survive the wound that he inflicts, and then, dear God, help me survive the desire to retaliate that is sure to follow. Help me forgive him as I did once before . . ."

Then he realized a lot of time had gone by. Too much. It doesn't take this long to crash that cane down. No blow had been struck, nothing had happened.

Watson opened his eyes and saw Tashimoto sitting calmly back down on the chair across from him. The cane was lying across his lap.

"A question, please," Watson said. "Did you pass on

what our guy said that day about Kyoto being the next target for an atomic bomb? Just curious."

"My wife and her family went to Kyoto when the awful
bombing of Tokyo began. They had heard you Americans
were going to spare Kyoto."

"I'm talking about what one of the prisoners said to you
about a third atomic bomb being dropped—"

"Be quiet! I know nothing about any such information."

Watson said nothing.

Tashimoto said, "You want to talk, we will talk. I will
talk now and you will listen.

"You choose to believe I am someone other than who I
am, but clearly I cannot change your mind. I am a Japanese
man named Tashimoto but not the one you had your unfortunate encounter with in World War II. But let me speak for
him, if I must. Let me speak for him and all of us who survived that terrible experience. Let me say that I regret any
harm and suffering that was inflicted on you unnecessarily
by anyone connected with the Imperial Army of Japan. But I
do not offer you an apology. I served in that army, and I
make no apologies to you or to anyone else for that service.
We served our emperor in an honorable and glorious way,
about which we should never feel ashamed. You want an
apology for what happened to you, well, Mr. . . . what did
you say your name was?"

"Watson. *Bishop* John Quincy Watson."

"Oh, yes. You were named for the sixth president of the
United States."

"Fifth."

The little man smiled. "Correct, Mr. Bishop Watson. I
was testing your knowledge of American history. Who was
the seventh?"

Watson looked away toward the Bay of San Diego. "Martin Van Buren," he said.

"Andrew Jackson is the correct answer. You should be

ashamed, Mr. Bishop. In Japan we are taught our history and we remember. We are also taught the history of the United States of America, and we remember. Have you ever been taught anything about Japan and the Japanese people?"

"I learned enough about the brutality of the Japanese people at Sengei 4 to last me two or three lifetimes, Mr. Fucky Duck."

"I would ask that you not call me by that offensive name. I have no idea where it comes from, but I do not like it. Please refrain from ever using it again in my presence."

"Please refrain from ever again giving orders in my presence."

Tashimoto whipped the cane down hard on the table between them. It made that same sharp, gunshot sound. "Be quiet! Listen to me!"

"Really like old times now, right? You with the bamboo stick, me your helpless, terrified prisoner."

"You must listen to what I say!"

"My hearing is terrible because of the banging you did on my ears, particularly the left one."

"I never banged on anything of yours! Shut up, you white American devil!"

Watson let out a screeching high-pitched laugh, as close as he could come to the one he heard too often from the Hyena of Sengei 4. Then he said to Tashimoto, "Gotcha. Tell me again about being at peace with what happened in the war."

Tashimoto seemed embarrassed, upset, lost.

Watson kept at him. "You try it," he said.

"Try . . . try what?"

"The laugh. Try your old laugh. Throw your head back and let it really go."

Watson laughed again in the best Hyena imitation he could manage.

Tashimoto's face cleared of confusion. He said, "You are a crazy old American fool, Mr. Bishop Watson."

"You are a crazy old Jap killer, Mr. Tashimoto."

Tashimoto shook his head and then repeatedly nodded, as if doing a quick exercise to clear things even more.

Then he said, "You call me a Jap killer. Let me talk to you about killers—Jap killers and American killers. What were you doing when you became a prisoner of the Imperial Army of Japan?"

"Flying an airplane."

"A B-29 bomber airplane?"

"Yes."

"What had you just done with your B-29 before you were captured?"

"We had dropped a load of bombs on Tokyo."

"What kind of bombs?"

"Incendiary bombs."

"Those are the ones that explode into fires that scatter across the ground and houses and people like liquid fire, turning every thing or person into ashes. Is that correct? What was your rank?"

"Lieutenant."

"Your assignment?"

"Pilot."

"Never in the course of the war did any Japanese pilot drop bombs on American civilians. No American city was bombed or destroyed. Never did a Japanese pilot set afire the houses and lives of American civilians. Not one American child or mother or grandmother was reduced to ashes by a Japanese bomb dropped from high above their city or town or farm or temple or school. Yes, we killed, we were killers of Americans. But we only killed American soldiers and sailors, and airmen like you who devastated our country. We did not kill innocents, we killed only the guilty."

The retired Methodist bishop of San Antonio knew that he was driving the other man and himself to a place where the Almighty would probably prefer they not go. But there was something in him—something that had nothing to do with the Almighty—that would not let him stop.

"We were guilty of nothing but defending ourselves against a nation of brutal beasts," Watson said.

"Brutal beasts! We are nothing of the kind! We are gentle, moral people. You Americans are the beasts; you are the devils whose racism against Asian people drove us to war. You are the devil who dropped the atomic bombs on our cities and brought nuclear horror to our world."

"It was what it took to get you maniacs to surrender. It was done to save lives—Japanese lives as well as American lives."

"You were the maniacal ones!"

Watson knew he should stop there and then. He knew this was a debate with no winner, a conflict with no ending, a story with no epilogue. But those words of peace and reconciliation he had spoken so many times in the last fifty years would not come again.

Tashimoto stood. He yelled, "You are the devils who have brought coarseness and filth and degradation to the Japanese people and all other people of the world. You and your terrible movies and television shows about serial murderers and sex fiends and heroin addicts. You are the ones brutalizing the rest of the world. How dare you call the Japanese people brutal beasts! We are the calming ones, the peaceful ones, the honorable ones of this world."

In his emotional anguish, Tashimoto let Watson's silver-headed cane fall to the floor.

Watson, moving as fast as he had in fifty years, reached over and grabbed it. "The worm turns again," he said. "Who was John Quincy Adams's vice president?"

"I believe it was . . . yes, it was Martin Van Buren."

"Nope. John Calhoun. Sit down, please."

He held the cane firmly but not menacingly. The Japanese man remained silent, crossing his legs and sitting down on the floor as he had before. That kind of move would have taken Watson several minutes to perform. Tashimoto did it quickly and made it look easy.

"Now I am going to talk and you are going to listen, Mr. Tashimoto," said Watson.

He sat back down in a chair across from Tashimoto and said, "As a point of fact and history, please try to remember—and never forget—that you Japanese started the war against us. You did so with a sneak attack. Please also remember—and never forget—that you set the pace and the standard of conduct for the war. You tortured and murdered prisoners of war from day one, and you were still doing it on day last. You were animals, and you turned others into animals. The level of brutality you people brought to the innocents of China and Korea alone is right up there with the most grievous and unforgivable in all of human history. Your soldiers raped their women and bayoneted and beheaded their children, starved their elderly. Do you at least acknowledge that? Do you at least know and understand what you people did to the Chinese and the Koreans?"

Tashimoto, head still bowed, acknowledged nothing, moved nothing.

"It would take an imagination beyond mine to even consider what you and your fellow Japanese might have done to Americans had you, by some work of the devil, won the war and conquered us. The thought of it brought not only terror to every American, it rallied them to an all-out industrial and personal war effort that finally brought us victory."

Tashimoto did not speak or move.

"What about the thousands of Filipinos you slaughtered? And the Australians and the British prisoners you turned into slaves and then worked to death on the Burma–Siam railroad? The truth was far worse than anything that was in the Alec Guinness movie."

There was still no sign the Japanese man had even heard what Watson said.

"And you got away with it," Watson continued. "You Japanese and your emperor got away clean. The total disregard for human life and dignity that you and your fellow soldiers brought to the war was beyond comprehension in a civilized world. That lack of comprehension worked to your advantage. Nobody could believe it happened. And there you sit with your legs crossed, a vice president of a big bank."

The retired bishop of San Antonio was not speaking in his pulpit bellow. He was using his quietly forceful voice, the one he used for small conferences, prayer groups, and the occasional television and radio interview.

He said to Tashimoto, "You should have been punished for your crimes, and until today I thought you had been. I would seriously like to know how you survived. I walked out of that shed—we all did—believing you were dead. Nobody, I don't think, actually tried to feel a pulse, but you certainly appeared dead. You certainly had had enough punishment to kill three men twice your size. How did you do it?"

Tashimoto raised his head and said in a near whisper, "I will not hear one more word from you. You are a man of lies and hate, Mr. Bishop Watson. I am also a Christian. I believe in forgiveness and other things good and noble and moral that you clearly do not. You are the monster in this room. You are the one who deserves punishment for crimes committed in the war.

"American marines committed wanton murder on Japanese prisoners on many of the islands where there was conflict. Our fine soldiers, captured in the line of duty, were tortured and maimed. Did you know about these crimes, Mr. Bishop? You Americans and your allies prosecuted our officers for war crimes after the war. Had the war ended differently, there would have been war-crimes trials of yours."

"I was not aware that any of our troops committed such atrocities against Japanese soldiers," Watson said.

Tashimoto was through talking. Again as swiftly and effortlessly as he had sat down, he uncrossed his legs and stood up. Watson rose to his feet, grasping the cane tightly in his right hand.

He saw the foot coming, but he simply could not react quickly enough this time. He dropped the cane and moved both hands toward his groin. They got there too late.

Watson's sexual reactions were numb down there, but not his ability to feel pain. He felt the force of Tashimoto's right foot as he had so many terrible times fifty years ago. The agony cracked through him like hot fireplace pokers.

He grabbed himself and bent over. "You bastard!" he bellowed.

He knew what was coming next—a kick under his chin to send him upright and sprawling backward. His rage sending strength through his body, Watson used the power in his good leg to push off toward Tashimoto.

His long arms and body extended, he dove onto the smaller man like a huge predatory bird on a tiny animal. Tashimoto fell straight back, with Watson on top of him.

Watson's face came to rest just above Tashimoto's. He felt the Japanese man's heavy breathing and smelled toothpaste and aftershave.

The retired bishop of San Antonio spoke not a word. Neither did the vice president of the First Nippon Bank of Tokyo.

His large body clearly in control, Watson grabbed Tashimoto's neck and head. He placed the right hand on the forehead, the other around behind, and in a quick motion, he snapped back the man's head.

When Watson heard the crack he knew he had just become a murderer for the third time.

Then he thought again. No.

Henry said this one wouldn't count.

CHAPTER TWELVE

He lay in a room at Brooke Army Medical Center in San Antonio, Texas.

He had been told that thus far he was the only one of the eleven crew members of *Big Red* who had turned up alive. The other ten were officially still missing.

He had been told he was suffering from acute malnutrition that was jeopardizing several internal body functions essential to normal life. His weight had shrunk to 129 pounds from 205 the last time he had been on a scale, which was at Smoky Hill Army Airfield in Kansas shortly before flying off to Saipan. The Brooke doctors said a careful regimen of special foods, given intravenously and through the mouth, plus regular exercise and other therapy might help him regain weight and reverse the damage.

He had been told that a decision would have to be made soon about his right leg. It was possible that a series of skin and muscle grafts could save it, but if not, it would have to come off—probably just below the knee.

He had been told that his penis, testicles, and scrotum were beyond repair. He would never again come or have an erection. While he would still most likely have erotic thoughts and reactions concerning women, it would be impossible for him to have sexual intercourse. This would have been devastating news under any circumstances, but for Watson it packed an extra wallop: He was a virgin, and now at age twenty he was being told that he always would be.

Now three military personnel came into his hospital room to ask him questions, the doctors having said it was finally all right for him to participate in the war-crimes interviews.

The officer in charge was a too-clean, too-young navy lieutenant-lawyer assigned to the Japanese War Crimes Commission. He reeked of purpose and Harvard. He was there with an army captain, also young and crisp, plus a silent, nervous WAC stenographer in her thirties who came with a notebook to take down every word in shorthand. They said the information Watson gave about his experiences as a prisoner of war would be used to investigate and prosecute all of those who ran Camp Sengei 4.

Watson was so tired and down he barely looked at them. He mostly listened.

"You were fortunate, Lieutenant," said the navy officer. "Only a handful—five percent total—of the B-29 crews captured by the Japs came out alive."

Fortunate? Me? Did he say I was fortunate?

The army captain said, "You were also lucky you weren't at one of the other Kempei Tai prisons—particularly at their headquarters in Tokyo. The B-29 boys there were kept chained and blindfolded in dungeons and old horse pens. They were beaten and tortured and starved—absolute barbarism. Few of them survived that. Many burned up in our own air raids because the Japs wouldn't let them out."

Lucky? I was lucky? Lucky fucky? What is lucky, Captain Fucky Duck?

"Let's get down to business," said the navy officer. "Who did this to you, Lieutenant?"

When Watson did not immediately answer, he said,

"Captain Henry Howell has given a statement saying the overwhelming majority of the atrocities and abuse was administered or ordered by a man you prisoners knew as the Hyena. We have identified him as T. Tashimoto, a native of Kyoto who was an officer in the Imperial Army of Japan's military police—the Kempei Tai. His official assignment was as an interpreter, but we understand he operated as an interrogator and, in most ways, as the leading force of the camp. Would you agree he was the person most responsible for the atrocities and abuse?"

Watson said he would.

"We have thus far been unable to locate and apprehend him," said the army captain. "Captain Howell claimed he couldn't help us. What about you? You don't happen to have any information on what happened to him, do you?"

Watson said he did not.

The navy man said, "We have in custody back in Japan two of the former enlisted guards at Sengei 4. One of them told our investigators that Tashimoto was kicked to death— essentially murdered—by some of the prisoners as the war was ending. He said he was sure two of the prisoners involved were tall Americans with red hair. Is that true, Lieutenant Watson? You are a tall American with red hair. So is Captain Howell."

Watson said he didn't know what the navy officer was talking about.

Then his whole body started shaking. He said to the Harvard-boy navy lieutenant and the army captain and the WAC's notebook that he didn't want to talk to them anymore about the Hyena or anything else.

They never came back, and neither did anyone else from the War Crimes Commission or any other official body interested in seeking justice for anything Watson did or had done to him at Sengei 4.

That actually didn't matter as much as it might have because Watson believed he had already had *his* justice.

.   .   .

Ten days later they gave Watson two medals. An Army Air Forces general wrote a letter to his mother and father in Connecticut inviting them to the award ceremony.

His folks had come to San Antonio to see him several times, but he was not able to be terribly welcoming or warm with them. His love for them was real and unabashed—they were all he had—but it worked against his bringing them into his private agonies, his raging anger. Why should they be made to suffer any more than they already had? Besides, his father, a good and quiet man of investments, was not the type to talk to about his son's permanent virginity. His mother would not have been good at helping decide whether to let them cut off half his leg. They were proud of their son and would have tried to do anything he asked, but he asked nothing of them. Maybe they were from a life that no longer existed. Their boy *had* died at Sengei 4.

Until the war was over, they had believed he really was dead. None of his captors had reported Watson as being a POW. All his parents received was a series of official messages from the U.S. government. First came a Western Union telegram from the army adjutant general saying: THE SECRETARY OF WAR DESIRES ME TO EXPRESS HIS DEEP REGRET THAT YOUR SON I/LT JOHN QUINCY WATSON HAS BEEN MISSING IN ACTION IN THE PACIFIC OCEAN AREA SINCE 19 FEB 45. IF FURTHER DETAILS OR OTHER INFORMATION ARE RECEIVED YOU WILL BE PROMPTLY NOTIFIED. A confirming letter came from Washington a few days later, followed by another, a month later, from the Presbyterian chaplain on Saipan. He told the Watsons that their son's plane had disappeared on a bombing mission over Tokyo. He wrote, "No one saw the plane crash and no one knows whether the men were able to bail out. If they were and are now prisoners of war, we cannot say. The situation may not seem too encouraging. But short of definite evidence, we should all hope that they may have been saved."

Watson's parents heard nothing else until a telegram came to their Westbrook home three weeks after V-J Day stating that the adjutant general was now pleased to inform them that their son had been liberated from a Japanese prison camp and would be on his way home soon.

The Watsons were there in the San Antonio hospital room the afternoon a handsome colonel with a black mustache came over from Randolph Field with a master sergeant to present the medals. Mr. Watson also had a mustache, but his was red like his hair. On this day he was wearing a charcoal-gray suit, a white shirt, and a dark blue tie. Mrs. Watson, fresh and blond, had on a yellow dress. It was hot that day in San Antonio, as it often was. Watson was concerned that his mom and dad would be uncomfortable as dressed up as they were.

The colonel first apologized for the medals not being of what he called "higher magnitude" than they were. "We feel assured, Lieutenant Watson, that your actions on your stricken aircraft that night over Tokyo were of a courageous and heroic level to justify the awarding of the Distinguished Flying Cross, if not something higher, such as the Silver Star. Unfortunately, there were no surviving witnesses to your actions because, as you know, you were the only member of your crew to survive the war. The wreckage of your plane has yet to be found, presumably because it's at the bottom of the Sea of Japan.

"At any rate, rules and procedures on those higher magnitude decorations require at least one witness in addition to the person himself."

So, said the colonel, all they could justify for Lieutenant Watson was an Air Medal for meritorious service as a B-29 pilot and a Purple Heart for the wounds inflicted while a prisoner of war.

Then, turning to Watson's parents, he said, "You have every right to be very proud of your son, Mr. and Mrs. Watson. Many were called upon in the war to rise beyond the call of duty. Your son did so. He is a true American hero. You should see this Air Medal and this Purple Heart as the highest citations this grateful nation can bestow on its sons."

As he pinned the two medals to Watson's nightshirt he said, "John Quincy Watson, Lieutenant, United States Army Air Forces: It gives me great pleasure on behalf of the president and the people of the United States to award you these decorations for your heroic service to your country and to the United States Army Air Forces."

Watson came within an embarrassing breath of saying, Thank you very much, Colonel Fucky Duck.

Mom and Dad would never have understood why their son—he had always been such a good boy—would say such a terrible thing at a time like this.

·   ·   ·

The Brooke doctors chose that evening of the medals to tell Watson that his right leg had to go. There was no longer any choice, they said. After painful and tedious surgery, grafting, and hope, it simply was not working.

The surgeon in charge said, "Sorry, Watson, I know how fond you've become of your lower right extremity, but its useful life is over. We must put it out of its misery before it makes your own misery much, much worse."

Watson pleaded for more time, another operation—anything but amputation. The doctor, an older Swede from Minnesota named Johannsen, pulled up the right leg of Watson's pajama bottoms to force the patient to see the awfulness for himself. Watson had done his best to avoid looking at the thing. Now he had to.

It was not a pretty sight. Below the knee, the limb resembled a plucked, uncooked chicken leg that had been ravaged by a coyote or some similar animal. A hyena maybe? The meat was dark red, streaked, raw, gnawed, and scabbed.

"That's mostly scar tissue," The doctor said. "There's very little muscle left in the calf, and we can't figure out a plausible way to graft in any more. We've already taken as much as I think we should from your back."

All right, but what if we just leave it the way it is?

"You'll be a cripple, and you'll probably hurt a little bit every day for the rest of your life."

Watson's nurse, a lieutenant in the army nurse corps named Joyce Landrum, also worked him over after the doctors left. She clearly agreed with Johannsen and the others about the need for the leg to be sawed off. Why hurt forever when you don't have to?

And then, almost as if on cue, they staged a show of quick-on/quick-off artifical legs, thinking that would make his decision easier. An expert on prosthetic limbs—a tech sergeant medic—came into the room to demonstrate his wares. There were legs for short people and tall people, some with knees, some without. Some were made of wood, others of steel, and there were some brand-new models in that relatively new stuff called plastic. Most had ankles and feet with movable parts designed to replicate the real things. Some, for display purposes, had colorful socks and shiny new shoes on the phony feet.

Watson watched and listened, as he had promised Joyce he would. But he asked no questions and declined all invitations to even hold one of the contraptions. He hated the idea of any part of him being artificial. The thought of putting on a

fake leg every morning with his own socks, shoes, underwear, and trousers was abhorrent. There was more to it than
that, of course. He had already lost the normal use of his sex
organs. Why voluntarily eliminate another vital piece of himself? He simply couldn't toss away a part of his body as if it
were trash.

But he was given no choice. It was going to happen at
0900 on a Friday morning in Operating Room 5C, Dr. Johannsen & Company doing the sawing. Watson would be
under ether and completely out of it when the small stainless
steel hacksaw was put to his right leg. Good-bye, vital piece.

"What happens to the cut-off part?" Watson asked at
0615 when Johannsen came by for a few last peppy words
before pre-op. It was a serious question.

"Nothing happens to it," said Johannsen, who definitely
did not see it as a serious question.

"So you really do just throw it away?"

"You wanted it sent to the Smithsonian or put on display
at a carnival or somewhere for schoolchildren to see?"

"I don't want it tossed."

"Okay. We'll put it in a very tall jar of formaldehyde so
you can have it as a souvenir to put on your fireplace mantel
or something. Happy now?"

A while later, when an anesthetist came to give the knockout ether, Watson told him to forget it. There would be no
operation this morning or any other morning.

Watson had expected Joyce Elisa Landrum, lieutenant,
USANC, to either cry or throw a tantrum. She did neither.
She simply shrugged, kissed her patient on the mouth, and
went off to tell Johannsen to stand down the operating-room
crew. It was a reaction that confirmed what the patient already pretty much knew.

This was the woman for him.

Joyce was not what most people would consider a pretty

woman. She was tall, and her nose was slightly large for her face, which was permanently scarred from childhood acne. Her legs were slightly bowed. She had grown up a high school principal's daughter in the East Texas town of Jasper and gone into the army nurse corps directly from nursing school at the University of Texas in Galveston just as the war was ending.

The first date she had in her life was when Watson asked her to accompany him—by pushing him in a wheelchair—to the hospital snack bar for a cold drink. They began as nothing more than a very sick and sad patient and a very bright and dedicated nurse, then it moved on to a favorite-patient/favorite-nurse relationship and, finally, to dependency and love. She washed him and fed him and, when both his arms were incapacitated with various tubes, even wiped him. She also bandaged him and stuck him with needles, read and wrote for him, listened to him, cried and suffered with him.

It was after the leg incident that he began to realize that he wanted to spend the rest of his crippled life with her.

They were married on a Saturday afternoon in the small chapel at Brooke. The service was conducted by Rick Allison, an army chaplain who had already become Watson's friend and was to play an important part in his religious life. Henry Howell, who had long since been discharged from the hospital, flew down from Boston to be the best man. Watson's parents were also there from Connecticut.

Joyce Landrum and Quincy Watson made a good fit. They were the same age—twenty-one. She was taller than 90 percent of the males she knew, and his six-four was ideal for her five-eleven. She was blond, and she claimed the romance magazines said blond women and redheaded men went together well and for a long time. Watson figured she made that up, but it didn't matter.

And there was the sex thing. As his nurse, Joyce knew

everything about Watson, including what had happened to his basic equipment. She already knew when he asked her to wheel him to the snack bar for a first date that there were acts of love that this man in the wheelchair could never perform.

He had already imagined some difficult and painful projections about asking a woman—*any* woman—to marry him. *Well, dear, before you say yes, there's something you may not have noticed: No matter what we do, I never get hard. What that means is that I cannot have intercourse with you when we are married. What* that *means is that we cannot have children of our own.*

He and Joyce did discuss openly and frankly what problems they would face under the sheets, to use Henry's term. They did manage to find—with the help of a sex therapist and some doctors—several new and creative techniques to fulfill some of their needs. They were not completely satisfying to either, of course.

The head of Brooke gave special permission for Joyce to spend their wedding night in Watson's hospital bed.

Watson told her he was so sorry he would never be able to really satisfy her.

"It beats the alternative," she said.

"What alternative?"

"Not being married to you."

He acted as if he didn't understand her.

"No need to deny our lovely, awful truth, Quincy," she said. "If you were not damaged, you would probably never give me a second look—and we wouldn't be in this bed together."

He did deny it, of course, strongly and sincerely.

CHAPTER THIRTEEN

John Quincy Watson, for the second time in his life, was electrified by killing a man—the same man. The blood was rushing through his veins, making his face flush and his heart pump faster than it had in years.

He returned to his chair and swiveled it away from Tashimoto to the sliding glass door, the balcony, and the San Diego Bay.

Watson knew he had to settle himself down. He tried hard to think of words he should say to himself—words he would speak, as a minister of the Lord, to someone else who had just killed another man with his own two hands, no matter what the reason.

He said out loud, "You committed this act—this violation of the seventh commandment against murder—in self-defense. This man, may his soul rest in peace, had just attacked you, as he had many years ago—"

Watson heard something. It was a human sound, a moaning. He turned around. Tashimoto's head was moving.

"Not again!" Watson shouted and limped over to the man on the floor. Tashimoto was not conscious, but he was clearly still alive. "Nobody survives a broken neck, Fucky Duck . . ."

Without even a split second's thought, Watson reached down, grabbed Tashimoto's right hand, and started pulling the moaning man toward the balcony.

Even though the body weighed only 130 pounds or so, Watson was exhausted by the time he arrived at the balcony's three-foot-high black iron hand railing. The sun had just gone down, but the beautiful purple of early evening still streaked the sky. A light breeze blew; the temperature was a perfect seventy degrees.

He sat down on one of the balcony chairs and took in the beauty of it all for a few minutes while he caught his breath.

Then, back on his feet and using most of his remaining strength, John Quincy Watson lifted the small body of the Japanese man up and over the railing, head first.

And let go.

The body fell straight down into the darkness eighteen floors below. Some people must have been sitting down there because Watson heard what he thought were shouts and screams.

Watson then went back inside to telephone Henry with the news.

CHAPTER FOURTEEN

If First Lieutenant Watson knew the oft-repeated quote of Jesus' in the New Testament on the subject of forgiveness—"Father, forgive them; for they know not what they do"—it meant nothing to him now, in the fall of 1945. Living through the hell of Sengei 4 and then trying to cope with the consequences on his body and soul afterward brought him to a very different form of those words: Forgive those little bastards nothing because they knew exactly what they were doing. Anybody who forgives them doesn't know what in the hell *he* is doing.

He said it that straight—and a lot less politely—when Rick Allison first came to call. Allison was a Methodist minister who went to war as a chaplain with Patton's Third Army Division in Europe, where he saw some severe combat and, as he said, heard some severe use of God's name in vain. He became skilled in the art of ministering to the terrified and the dying, and that expertise, most particularly with the postcombat depressed and the suicidal, caused the army to ask him to briefly delay his own discharge in order to help some of the most seriously scarred. That was what he was doing at Brooke.

He worked mostly with the men who couldn't handle survival. They included a master sergeant who couldn't sit down for more than ten minutes at a time. So he walked and walked around the hospital, talking occasionally but mostly just walking, almost all day and night. There was another man—he had been locked up in a cage for three months outside Manila—who could not bear for the door—*any* door on which he was on the other side—to be closed.

Watson wasn't that bad. He wasn't even suicidal, being too grateful to be alive for that. And he probably wasn't what would later be called clinically depressed. It was his extreme case of the hates that caused the army psychiatrists and psychologists, having thrown up their hands, to dispatch Rick Allison to see if God could come up with a cure.

The shrinks had warned him every day, sometimes more than once, that his major problem beyond walking and sex was going to be dreaming. One of the gloomier forecasts was that it might be five years—or even ten or more—before he closed his eyes and slept the night through without seeing and feeling and screaming over what little Japs were doing to him and others.

He did have terrible dreams about the kicks and whacks, the corpses and executions. But he also had a few about the little Japs' own suffering from the firebombs he and other Americans had dropped. The worst one involved a real Japanese man Watson had seen from a moving truck in Tokyo after being liberated from Sengei 4. The man, standing alone near some bombed-out ruins, seemed barely alive. His hair was gone, his skin was raw, his eyes glowed with hate.

Watson relived the death of the Hyena repeatedly, and those relivings were the delicious highlights of his nights. A new orderly, a corporal who was not yet accustomed to Watson's sleeping habits, shook him out of such a scene late one night.

"Hey, Lieutenant, I can't tell if you're happy or sad," he said. "But whatever, you're so loud they're hearing you in Chicago."

"What was I doing?"

"I don't know what you were doing in the dream, but you were making a sound that was somewhere between a screaming ninny and a guy being jerked off by Lana Turner." The corporal had it about right. That was pretty much how the dreams felt—particularly those about the Hyena.

Those dreams branched out into imagined executions of other Japanese, some of whom Watson knew, some he didn't. He saw the faces of a variety of Japanese men, from Emperor Hirohito and General Tōjō, the villainous commander of the Japanese military, on down the chain of command and life, going to their deaths by torture and abuse. Most times Watson was the happy administrator of the beheadings, the torture and the abuse by water, bamboo sticks, fists, kicks, and rifle and pistol butts. On more than one occasion he administered death by strangulation with a short piece of rope.

Watson recounted each episode in great detail to the sympathetic army shrinks, who shook their heads with shock and concern, especially over his cackling enjoyment of these awful dreams. But they pretty much had nothing to offer in the way of assistance or a cure. Only time.

And Rick Allison.

Allison was definitely no grinny, sweet-mouthed preacher boy spouting platitudes. He came from the get-tough school of preachers who spoke in hear-this, no-choice terms about God, *His* will as well as *your* will. He had been an All Big Eight fullback/linebacker at the University of Colorado before he went to divinity school. He wore his hair in a crew cut and maintained a weight lifter's toned and bulging muscles. His opinions and reactions he kept right out front.

He was known around the hospital for his total lack of

sympathy for whining. He believed—yelled, in some cases—that each person is in control of his own life. Blame yourself or blame no one. Take charge or shut up.

When he came to see Watson he already knew about the Hyena and most of the Sengei 4 story and he immediately used the worst of it against Watson.

"How is participating in a group murder, kicking a defenseless man to death, any different than what was done to you?" he asked.

"If you don't see the difference, then there's no way to explain it."

Allison fired right back. "You're the one who doesn't see the difference, Lieutenant Watson. Your guilt, which you're too he-man to admit, has you all wrapped up in so many knots you can't get this out of your system."

"Bullshit!"

"Say it because your mouth is full of it."

And it went on like that for hours, days, weeks.

I have no guilt!

You reek of it like garlic.

I have nothing to be guilty about!

What about firebombing women and children and old men?

I was only doing my job!

What about the Hyena?

The little shit deserved to die!

You are designated by God to make such decisions?

God wasn't at Sengei 4.

Oh, yes, he was.

The most traumatic and difficult hurdle for Watson was to think and talk straight about simply having survived when so many others did not. He was the only one of his B-29 crew. He and Henry Howell were among only a small number of American flyers who came home from Japanese captivity.

Rick worked and worked on Watson to admit that guilt—survivor's guilt, he called it—which scarred the soul within his maimed body. He said guilt was one of the major things that distinguished us humans from all lower species of life. A coyote kills an innocent rabbit—Rick was from Alamogordo, New Mexico—and feels absolutely no remorse. Neither does the shark who eats a sunfish, a rattlesnake who swallows a baby chick, a dog who bites a baby girl.

"Face it, Watson. A person who kicks another human being to death and feels no remorse has got a problem," said Rick. "So does one who turns babies into toast from five thousand feet. And so does a guy who doesn't understand why God chose him to live while so many others died." Rick put these points to him—and put them and put them—until Watson quit yelling back.

And Rick always circled back to forgiveness, claiming that was the single strongest cleansing agent we have as God's creatures. He said the power to give and accept forgiveness was the supreme power of civilized man. He said there is no person on the face of the earth who does not have the need to forgive and to be forgiven.

It was while he was on forgiveness that he began to quote people Watson had never heard of—theologians Niebuhr and Tillich, a psychiatrist named Frankl. They were people Rick considered modern and worth really studying.

Viktor Frankl's just-published writings about man's ability to withstand the worst possible conditions and horrors were particularly relevant. His conclusion, based on his experience in Nazi concentration camps, was that a search for meaning is the primary motivation of human beings. "There is nothing in the world, I venture to say, that would so effectively help one to survive even the worst conditions as the knowledge that there is a meaning to one's life." To that Watson eventually said amen.

He also tried to say amen to Frankl's helpful thoughts about dealing with survivor's guilt, a problem that inflicted Frankl himself and many others who survived the Holocaust. Why me? Watson asked. Why *not* Southie or Owens or Parish or the other good men of *Big Red*? Or Lederer or Wiley or the kid from Tulsa or the many other good men of Sengei 4?

Watson got no satisfying answers from Frankl or anybody else.

On forgiveness, Watson did better. From Frankl and the others, Rick took Watson directly to the Bible and to Christianity, which, according to Rick, pretty much invented the concept of personal forgiveness.

There was that best-known quote from Luke, and others from the New Testament. From Mark: "Whenever you stand praying, forgive, if you have anything against anyone; so that your Father in heaven may also forgive you your trespasses." From Romans: "Blessed are those whose iniquities are forgiven, and whose sins are covered; blessed is the one against whom the Lord will not reckon sin." And from Colossians: "Bear with one another and, if anyone has a complaint against another, forgive each other; just as the Lord has forgiven you, so you also must forgive."

Watson listened and read and talked and, finally, began— ever so slowly—to consider his own needs to both forgive and to be forgiven. He argued for a while with Rick about the absurdity of granting forgiveness to the Japanese when they hadn't even asked for it because they wouldn't even admit they had done anything wrong. Rick said forgiveness of or by a nation was meaningless. If it wasn't personal, it meant nothing.

Their conflict came to a head one night in a new nightmare, one that was very different from the others.

He was in the corpse shed with Henry Howell and Jack

Lederer and a small U.S. Army band. The musicians were playing "Stars and Stripes Forever," but Watson could not remember the words, so he sang along the words of "Jesus Loves Me." There were naked bodies of dead men everywhere. Some had smooth skin that had turned dark blue or light green. Others were lily white or covered with bruises or blood. Some of them were headless or legless, some were covered with rats or maggots, some had their eyes open staring straight up. All had nothing but bloody messes in their crotches. Some had the faces of an Australian commando, some had curly red hair. There in the middle of the room was the Hyena down on his knees with his head on the wooden block that was covered with dirt from having been buried. Standing behind the Hyena was a thin Japanese man wearing thick glasses and an elaborate uniform. It was Emperor Hirohito. In his two hands he held a sword, which he raised up over his head and brought down against the Hyena's neck. Nothing happened—there was no blood. The head stayed connected to the neck. The blade was bent as though it was rubber.

The band members started screaming about an atomic bomb coming, and they dropped their instruments and ran away. The Hyena stood up, faced the emperor, bowed, and took the rubber sword from him. "Watson!" he screamed. Watson tried to take a step toward him, but his feet wouldn't move. Jack Lederer started over toward the Hyena despite Henry's trying to hold him back. Lederer grabbed the sword out of the Hyena's hands and cracked it across the Jap's face, cutting off the top of his head and knocking him to his knees. The sword wasn't rubber after all. Henry kicked the Hyena and so did Watson and all the corpses. The Australian commando kicked Watson in the groin.

Suddenly there was fire coming down from the ceiling. The Hyena grabbed Watson around the legs, his topless head coming barely to Watson's knees. He hugged Watson tight and said, "I forgive you, Fucky Duck, because you know not what you do." Watson kicked him away. The Hyena clung to Watson. Watson kicked him again, again, again . . .

Watson woke up, determined to forgive.

CHAPTER FIFTEEN

Henry answered the phone on the first ring. "It's been over an hour, Quincy," he said. "Why in the hell didn't you call?"

"I've been busy."

"I tried to find you. I've been calling every goddamn hotel in San Diego looking for a Tashimoto."

"This is the Hotel Bayfront. It's quite nice, actually. What's the problem? I'm only ten minutes late calling."

"Quincy, that guy there in San Diego is *another* Tashimoto."

John Quincy Watson, standing with the help of his cane, was talking on the phone by the bed in Tashimoto's room. He sat down on the edge of the bed. His breathing became difficult.

Howell said, "I called the tracking service that Brady Wilson started years ago. You remember Brady, the professional POW? Brady's dead, but one of his sons still operates it. They've got everybody on computer—the prisoners like us, and the Jap bad guys like Tashimoto. They have a clean verification that our Tashimoto—the Hyena himself—really did die that day in the shed. He really was from Kyoto, and we really did kill the little shit. That guy with you could be one of two other Tashimotos still on the computer bad list. Both were Jap officers accused but never even arrested much less tried or convicted of anything. Of course! Few of them were. One did his dirty work as a company commander in China, the other as an interpreter type in Singapore."

Quincy did not respond. He could not respond. His mouth would not move.

"Quincy, for chrissake, what's going on? Did you hear what I said? Talk to me."

Watson, after a couple of minutes, was able to talk. "Was the one at Singapore named *Bill Joe* Tashimoto?"

"Let me look. Yes. Bill Joe was the Singapore guy. Strange name for a Jap, isn't it? Must be from a very mixed marriage—a redneck daddy from Houston, maybe, and a Jap mama from Kyoto—"

"I did what you said, Henry. I killed him. I killed that Bill Joe Tashimoto. You said they'd give me a medal."

"Jesus, Quincy!"

"Don't use His name like that!"

"Oh, please. We've been through this a thousand times. I'm a Catholic, and I can use his name any damned way I please."

"Sorry. Not the time for that. Not the time for that. I just murdered an innocent man. I just threw an innocent man off a hotel balcony."

The silence on the telephone seemed to go on forever.

Finally Henry said in a soft voice, "Well, well, Quincy, and so be it. Tell me what happened."

"You're not going to believe what I'm going to tell you, Henry. *I* don't believe what I'm going to tell you."

Watson told the story. When he was finished, Henry asked, "Did you check the man's walk, Quincy? That should have been a clue that he was the wrong Tashimoto."

"I forgot the walk. The eyes were his, I swear. I knew those eyes."

Howell asked Watson what he planned to do now.

"Turn myself in to the police," said Watson.

Howell said, "Good. I'll make some calls and find you a lawyer, and then Henry junior and I will be on the next plane for San Diego." Henry's son was a Boston lawyer who specialized in criminal law.

They hung up and Watson called 911. An official voice—female—told him to wait right there in the room until the police arrived.

Watson walked back out to the balcony. There were sounds of sirens approaching and of people down below, all now part of a tragedy that he had created. Those people made him think of the publicity and the television cameras and a trial that was now going to be his immediate life.

He thought that it was not possible for him to have done what he must have done.

Then he thought of being a prisoner again.

And that made him remember Jackson Wiley, the gentle music man from Nebraska who woke up every morning at Sengei 4 shaking with intense fear and dread of what lay ahead that day. Then one morning he didn't open his eyes. Jackson Wiley had willed himself dead.

Watson considered trying that now. But he quickly realized that the intensity of his desire to die wasn't strong enough to get the job done the Jackson Wiley way.

There had been those others at Sengei 4 who took their own lives by hitting a Japanese guard, making an obvious and clumsy run to escape, or doing something else that they knew would bring automatic death. That method was not available on this hotel balcony either.

That left only direct action.

He leaned his cane against the railing and gradually began lifting his scarred, lame right leg up over the top. His pant leg inched up, and in the light coming from the sitting room he got a glimpse of this limb that he had refused to throw away, fifty years ago.

"No!" he bellowed.

He lowered his leg and in his quiet, firm voice said, "No, Watson. No. You will not do this."

II

So Long

CHAPTER SIXTEEN

He had visited Henry's island home on Martha's Vineyard several times but always to play, to rest, to relax. And he had come as himself, as the good preacher guest of his good judge friend.

This time he was there to escape—to hide, to wait, to wonder.

And he came as somebody else—the war-crazed vet who had murdered a man.

When Watson looked at his reflection in water and windows and mirrors or saw his police mug shot or other photographs in print or on television he wondered who, oh Lord, is that? What happened to that other man, the man of peace and grace, who had put behind him the hurts of fifty years ago and the people who'd inflicted them?

At first he had denied he was what he was, that he had done what he had done. *There is no way I, John Quincy Watson, could break a man's neck with my own two hands and then, to finish the job, toss him off a hotel balcony. Not me, not this good man of God.*

The denials were not made formally to detectives or magistrates or lawyers in San Diego—they were made only to himself. What he had said to others as he went through the initial humiliation of arrest, exposure, and arraignment were words of confession, remorse, and bewilderment.

How could I have done such an awful thing? I don't know.

What snapped? I don't know.

Had a long-dormant barbaric monster been waiting in his soul all this time? I don't know.

I don't know, I don't know.

Henry Howell, Jr., and the San Diego lawyers on the case had urged Watson to think and speak only of self-defense, of reflexive reaction. A man is attacked in a horrible manner with a kick to his privates; he reacts. Wouldn't anyone do the same thing? Particularly if he had lived through your special hell in the Hyena's Japanese prison camp?

But Watson had never uttered any of those defending words to anyone. He did not believe them. He did not believe he couldn't have helped himself, that he had no choice but to kill Bill Joe Tashimoto.

How could a normal, civilized child of God do such a thing? That was the only question that really mattered, and it was one that John Quincy Watson could not answer.

All he had said publicly was this: "It is impossible to adequately put into words the deep sorrow I feel. I wish I could offer suitable consolation to the family of Mr. Tashimoto. All I can offer them is my full and unequivocal remorse. I wish I could rationalize it to my God. All I can do is pray to Him for forgiveness. I wish that I could explain it to my fellow and sister Methodists in Texas and elsewhere who have given me their faith and support for so many years. I cannot. To them and to others, including the authorities of San Diego and the state of California, I say that I stand ready to deal with the consequences of my horrendous act.

"And I say to everyone: Pray for me if you wish, but please offer me no sympathy, no pity. Do not see me as a victim. Bill Joe Tashimoto and his family are the only victims in this case. Thank you."

Watson had read those words into a gaggle of microphones, cameras, and reporters in front of the San Diego County Courthouse upon release from jail the day after the killing. In the new media world of twenty-four-hour cable news, the story had been an immediate sensation. A respectable Methodist bishop taking revenge on the man he thought was his World War II torturer was good copy by itself. But the dramatic method of the death (there were endless slow-motion videotape re-creations of the path of the body's fall from the eighteenth floor) plus the prospect of a murder trial with a war-crimes angle had moved it into the category of all-out coverage.

Watson had taken no questions after reading his statement and had said nothing publicly since, despite the pleas from hundreds of news organizations and some of the nation's leading and most charming TV anchors and interviewers. He had ordered his lawyers to keep quiet as well, which was certainly no problem for Henry junior, who believed in trying lawsuits in courtrooms, not in the press, and who had given the San Diego lawyers on the team a harsh warning against seeing this case as an audition to be a cable talk-show host. This may be California, he told them, but this defense is not.

Watson had spent only the night of the killing in jail and a total of twenty hours in police custody. There was enough that was commendable in his background and enough mitigating circumstances in his crime to convince the presiding judge at the arraignment to free him on bond until trial. And so he had flown with Henry the next day to hide out on Martha's Vineyard.

They walked the beach together early every morning before having a quiet breakfast.

"Who was it who killed himself by just strolling out into the waves?" Watson asked Henry the first day as they stepped along the narrow strip of dark sand that zigzagged around the island of lush greenery and, increasingly, large summer homes.

"A guy in a Marquand short story—or maybe it was by Cheever or Salinger," Henry replied. "I think *fish* was in the title—or maybe it was *tuna*."

The water was rough and dark that morning, and so was the April sky. Watson, because of his right leg, was not much of a beach person, particularly in hot Texas, where walking down a white-sand Gulf beach in long pants would have been considered eccentric. But up here, where the sand was brown and the temperatures cool, it wasn't a problem. He felt comfortable and normal walking along in khaki trousers and a Harvard sweatshirt borrowed from Henry.

"I mean a real person," Quincy said. "A famous woman poet, maybe?"

"Jeanne would have known."

Watson agreed without having to say so. Of course Jeanne, Henry's late wife, would have known. She was a psychotherapist who specialized in the treatment of women under stress. She was also one of the best-read people Watson had ever known.

Henry said, "If you're thinking about doing something like that, forget it." He picked up a small rock and with great gusto threw it out into the waves.

"I almost followed Tashimoto over the balcony the other night," Watson said.

"That possibility occurred to me. Then I figured, no way. Not Quincy. A man doesn't survive what he has survived and then throw away his own life."

Watson laughed. "You know me all right."

Henry stopped and looked right at Watson. "The problem

for me is that I'm not so sure I know myself. I'm not sure what I would have done in that hotel room. I might have killed him even if he hadn't kicked me in the balls."

"You told me on the phone to—"

"Forget what I told you on the phone. I wasn't there with the man, you were. The idea of that sadistic, barbaric little shit still being alive and here he is . . . well, I don't know what I think."

"What happened at Sengei 4 is a part of us, Henry, as much as our hair and our beliefs. We thought once it was over it was over. It was never over and never will be."

They started walking again.

"I'm worried about you being a prisoner again, Quincy, to tell you the truth," Henry said after a couple of minutes. "I don't think I could do it."

"That's why I almost went over the balcony."

"Henry junior's a good lawyer. He'll keep you free without you having to jump off any balconies or walk out into the waves . . . Virginia Woolf."

"What about her?"

"She was the one who did the walking."

Yes, yes, Quincy thought. There had been a play about Virginia Woolf several years ago that he and Joyce had gone to see at a theater in San Antonio. They went because the director was the daughter of a parishioner.

He looked out at the crashing waves, which were only slightly lighter than the water and the sky.

And he wished so much that this was only a scene from a play about John Quincy Watson.

.   .   .

It was a debate between sons about justice for fathers.

"There must be a trial!" Doug Wilson said. "The American public must hear the bishop's story!"

"Bullshit," said Henry junior.

They had just sat down with Watson and Henry senior at a table in La Siena, an upscale Italian restaurant in the Gaslight section of downtown San Diego. Henry senior had heard the place had great linguini pesto, his favorite pasta, and several Chianti wines that were rare and special.

"We must not let them sweep this under the rug again," Wilson said. "For the sake of everyone who died, you mustn't make a deal."

"That is a goddamn outrageous thing to say!" said Henry junior. "That decision will be made in accordance with what is best for Bishop Watson. We are not running some Japan payback public relations campaign here."

Doug Wilson's late father, Brady Wilson, had been a survivor of the Bataan Death March, considered the worst atrocity committed by the Japanese against Americans in the war. After the fall of the Philippines to the Japanese in April 1942, some 18,000 U.S. and Filipino POWs died during a long, brutal forced march across central Luzon, the Philippines' largest island, to an overcrowded outdoor prison camp, where thousands more died. From his home in Los Angeles, Brady had single-handedly organized a nationwide Japanese POW survivors' association right after the war. When his father died seventeen years ago, Doug, while going on with his regular life as a stockbroker, took over the dwindling crusade to extract recognition and compensation for what he called the forgotten ones—the Americans who had suffered as prisoners of the Japanese.

The issue on the well-set table tonight was whether to enter into serious plea bargain negotiations with the district attorney of San Diego County. A deal would mean quick disposition with no trial, no further publicity. Henry junior and the California lawyers on the defense team believed they could negotiate a very light prison sentence, possibly even probation for Bishop Watson.

The two young debaters—both were in their late thirties—
could not have been more different. Doug Wilson was hot:
skinny, red-faced, short, and bald. Henry junior was cool:
tall, husky, dark blond, and low-key.

"This is a criminal-justice matter involving what is known
as homicide—murder," said Henry junior as his father and
friend Quincy Watson went about the business of dinner,
holding a whispered consultation between themselves over
the wine list. "The issue is justice and freedom for Bishop
Watson."

"What about justice for Bishop Watson and your father
and my father for what was done to them fifty years ago?"
said Doug Wilson.

"Then and now are not connected to each other under the
goddamn criminal laws of California."

"They are under the goddamn laws of humanity."

"This is a goddamn murder case."

"It's also a goddamn atrocity case."

"Wrong! It is no such thing!"

Wilson said, "Our files have some pretty good stuff—
clues, indications, at least—that Bill Joe Tashimoto may
have been as bad in Singapore as the Hyena guy was at the
bishop's and your dad's camp."

"That's irrelevant unless we can prove it," Henry junior
said.

The bishop, after first insisting that their waiter be allowed to take their orders, felt compelled to enter the fray to
end this dispute. "I think Mr. Tashimoto's personal history
is irrelevant no matter how bad it might have been and even
if it can be proved. I killed the wrong man, but it's all right
because he deserved to die anyhow? No, thanks."

"Sometimes you have to take what you can get, Quincy,"
Henry senior reasoned.

"We're still working on proving what Bill Joe Tashimoto
did at Singapore," said Doug Wilson.

"He told me he was a good man," the bishop said. "There is no reason to believe otherwise. Leave his memory alone."

"Tōjō would probably have told you he was a good man, too." said Doug. "There's even a new movie coming out in Japan that says as much—it's called *Pride,* if you can believe it."

Watson and Henry senior had flown to San Diego two days before, slipping into the city unnoticed by almost everyone except Doug Wilson, who had been lying in wait. He found them at their hotel, a Sheraton. Wilson had insisted on being heard and had promised not to leave any of them alone until he got his hearing. Thus this dinner.

Watson was not that interested in the young man's pitch for a public airing of the Japanese POW cause. Neither was Henry senior. Fifty years ago they lived and passed through the first angry period when their collective stories seemed to be an embarrassment to the victorious generals. That was most particularly true of Douglas MacArthur, whose bad decisions about the Philippines had led to many Americans becoming POWs in the first place. But others in subsequent White House administrations and the Congress had had similar reactions. They wanted to move on, first in peace and then, almost immediately, into a cold war against Stalin and the Russians. They needed the Japanese in that war.

Doug Wilson was annoyed, almost angry, at how little Henry junior seemed to know about what had happened during the war as well as afterward. In a high-pitched staccato, he ran through a litany of specific atrocities that occurred during the Bataan Death March and at prison camps and aboard ships—the so-labeled Ships of Death.

"An American army captain could not keep up with his group of marching prisoners. He was shot in the head but not killed, and a group a prisoners immediately behind him was forced to march right over the downed and bleeding man . . .

"On Palawan Island in the Philippines, Japanese soldiers herded one hundred and fifty American prisoners into air-raid shelters and then poured gasoline on top and set a fire. When the prisoners came running out to escape the killing heat, they were machine-gunned, clubbed, or bayoneted to death . . .

"The conditions on those ships were barbaric, driving prisoners mad enough to drink blood and urine and to kill one another. Of the estimated fifty thousand prisoners put on ships, nearly eleven thousand died at sea . . ."

Wilson raved on. And Henry junior seemed to be listening. Watson watched but didn't really listen. He had already known and forgotten all this, and he had no interest in refreshing his memory.

His thoughts were about these two sons. There was this kid Doug Wilson fighting his father's fight. There was the other kid, Henry junior, trying to represent his father's friend's interests. A feeling of deep self-pity came rolling over Watson. It was an emotion he had worked at most of his life since Sengei 4 to avoid. But now it came through him in the form of nausea and then some slight watering in his eyes. The sons. He had no sons, no daughters—no children, no grandchildren.

He and Joyce had discussed adopting, but they'd never gotten around to doing anything about it, primarily because there was so much in their lives to do without children. It had only been since Joyce's death and his retirement that Watson began to miss what he had never had—someone besides Joyce to really love and to really love him. Brady Wilson had—and even in death still has—Doug. Henry has Henry junior . . .

Watson, distraught and embarrassed by his sadness, tried to focus on what Doug was saying, to get his mind off himself.

But that was even worse. The advocate son had moved on

from atrocity stories to reciting numbers. Nearly twelve thousand Americans—more than half of those captured by the Japanese—did not survive captivity. Only 5 percent of the special prisoners, the U.S. airmen captured by the Japanese, came out alive. That compared with a 96 percent overall survival rate for American prisoners held by the Germans! And so on. And nobody cared—or cares—and so on.

Wilson, noting that the bishop appeared to be paying attention again, said, "Bishop Watson, let me say it again directly to you: As unfortunate as the death of that Tashimoto may be for you personally, it presents an opportunity to finally settle some scores for you, Mr. Howell, my father, and all others who suffered as prisoners at the hands of the Japanese in World War II. This Tashimoto was as bad as the other one. They are both part of an untold story, Bishop. It's a crime against humanity that humanity has thus far mostly ignored or swept under the rug for political reasons."

Henry senior, who, like Watson, had remained mostly silent, fixed on sipping his wine and eating his pasta, told Wilson to give it a rest. It was over fifty years ago. Time heals, time forgets.

"Wrong, sir!" Wilson insisted. "There was a story in the *L.A. Times* the other day about the Japanese cabinet minister who laid a wreath at the war memorial in Yasukuni. One of those honored is Tōjō! *Tōjō!* He was convicted and hanged as a war criminal! It was his policy to annihilate and abuse war prisoners! It would be like having a statue of Adolf Hitler in downtown Berlin that Helmut Kohl goes by to pay his respects! But it would never happen in Germany. Never. The Jews would never stand for it. But in Japan, no problem. Too bad there were no Jews in the Philippines, at Bataan or Corregidor, on the Burma–Siam railroad. At Yasukuni they even have an old steam engine honoring the building of that railroad. Thousands of POWs and Asian civilians were used as slave labor on that wretched project—more than ten thousand of them died. It's all so outrageous, and nobody cares . . ."

Doug refocused his preaching on Henry junior. That was because the two older men had been suddenly distracted by a handwritten note that a waiter had delivered to Bishop Watson from another restaurant patron.

It said, "All of America stands behind you, Bishop. You look much more handsome in person than on television news. I would love to have you by my house for a drink later this evening or for dinner and other pleasures any other time. I can only imagine what it must have been like to be shot down and captured by the Japanese."

A signature and a local telephone number followed.

The bishop—with Henry—looked around the restaurant to see a black-haired woman waving delicately in his direction. She appeared to be in her fifties and was most attractive.

.   .   .

"Are you going to call her?" Henry senior asked the second they sat down.

"No," Watson replied.

"You idiot."

It was just after six-thirty the next morning, and they were off in a corner of the Sheraton coffee shop preparing to eat breakfast, which had always been the two old friends' favorite meal to have together. Henry had called down ahead of time to ask for a table as isolated as possible. There were not only reporters and cameras to contend with but also other people—*real* people as distinguished from journalists, according to Henry—who wanted to get a word, a look, or some other acknowledgment from America's newest celebrity killer, the retired Methodist bishop of San Antonio.

Their waitress, for instance, immediately asked for an autograph. A Hispanic woman in her thirties, she asked shyly, "Oh, Bishop, please, would you mind signing your menu for me? My husband's a Catholic, but he thinks you're innocent and a hero."

"He's both," said Henry. "He'll sign it but on one condition—that you keep everyone else away from us while we eat. I'll have the cheese omelet, hash browns, Canadian bacon, a large glass of orange juice, and coffee, black."

Watson wrote, as instructed, "To Michael Aleman—all the best, Quincy Watson" across the front of the large cardboard menu and ordered a toasted sesame bagel, half a grapefruit, and a cup of tea.

The coffee shop was huge and noisy, with that shiny cookie-cutter feel of hotel coffee shops everywhere. The tables were chrome and light blue Formica, their tops crowded with silverware, glass salt and pepper shakers, crocks holding packs of sugar substitute, and metal stands featuring colored cards advertising pepperoni pizza and other all-day specials. In an hour they were to meet the sons to talk more about plea bargain strategy. Final decision time was approaching.

But Henry wanted to talk about sex.

Watson didn't. "Here I am charged with murder. And what would you have us do? Sit here like two old farts and talk about a mash note from some stranger across a crowded room."

Henry replied, "Repeat after me, Quincy. We are not old farts. We are not too old to talk about mash notes. Call the woman, goddamn it. She's hot for your deformed, dilapidated old body."

"She wouldn't be if she knew the exact condition of said body," said Watson.

"She knows, Quincy. Everybody knows. It's been in the

newspapers and on every low-class cable-television program in America. Everybody in America knows you can't get a hard-on. Think about *that*, Bishop. Think about that for being a celebrity. Look around this coffee shop. Just think—everybody in here knows that you have not had an erection in fifty years."

It was all Watson could do to keep from laughing hysterically—like a hyena, say—at this glorious man across the table from him.

They had emerged from their prisoner experience bonded forever, as deeply as any two blood brothers could be. Henry had come out of Sengei 4 with less damage to his body and had left Brooke after only sixty days, during which he was mostly fattened up. He already had an undergraduate degree. So with all engines running, he went right to Harvard Law School, had a brilliant career as a tax lawyer in Boston, and through connections to the Kennedy political machine became a federal district judge. Along the way he married a beautiful Boston Brahmin heiress and produced six children, Henry junior being the eldest.

Henry and Watson had stayed in steady touch through letters and phone calls and occasional visits back and forth. They saw each other more after Watson became bishop because he was often invited to the Boston area to preach or attend large church meetings. In the first several years after the war, whatever way they communicated about anything, their shared horror and rage about Sengei 4 were always right there. And while both had been unresponsive to Doug Wilson's preaching at the restaurant, they felt there were things to be said about it. But these things would be said in private to each other.

"All that kid Wilson needs is a Steven Spielberg to make a *Schindler's List* movie or TV miniseries about the Jap stuff," Henry said.

"Better in a movie than in my trial."

"Maybe so, maybe not. The kid brought some of the heat back, didn't he, Quincy?"

"A little here and there." Watson's grapefruit had arrived.

"Like what?" Henry was already into a second glass of orange juice.

"Like do you still not eat Japanese food or drink sake or Japanese beer?"

"No way. You?"

"Same. It's out of habit now rather than . . . well, any kind of protest."

"I remember when you bought your first Japanese car."

"Right. A Nissan. Great little car."

"I ragged you. Hell, I remember feeling strange when I bought a Sony TV."

They had talked about these things over the years. Including the fact that while Watson had traveled on church business throughout Asia—China, South Korea, Thailand, even Singapore—he had yet to set foot on an island of Japan and probably never would. He and Henry particularly had no interest in going on one of those trips organized for former POWs to see where it had all happened to them.

Neither much followed the news—political or otherwise—from or about Japan, although Watson did take joyful notice when Henry Howell called one day in 1988 to report that Emperor Hirohito had finally died.

"You're the lawyer, Henry," Watson had said that evening. "Why did they let him completely off the hook?"

Henry had only mumbled something about politics. At the time there was no other answer that would have made sense to either Watson or Henry.

Some things still didn't make sense. Now, as Henry tasted his omelet, Watson said, "I watched—by accident, really—a rerun of that old TV sitcom about a German prison camp the other night."

"*Hogan's Heroes,* I remember it. It still pisses me off that somebody could find that kind of crap funny."

"Me, too. And it surprised me that I still felt that way."

"Isn't it interesting that no creative genius ever wrote a comedy about Japs beheading captured American flyboys?"

Then they laughed as they remembered their favorite piece of old news. The story of Lieutenant Marcus McDilda, a U.S. Army Air Forces fighter pilot who was shot down and captured shortly after the bombing of Hiroshima. He told his Japanese interrogators that he knew all about the atomic bomb and for hours passed on minute details about its makeup and design—and that Tokyo was on the list to be bombed next. It was all lies, but he told them so convincingly that the information was transmitted to the so-called Big Six, the Japanese war cabinet calling the shots from an underground shelter in Tokyo. The magazine story suggested that the information helped convince some of the leaders to surrender.

"My cooked-up hokum with Larson about Kyoto was not so far-fetched as it seemed at the time," said Henry.

But there was a haunting postscript to the McDilda story that also bore directly on Watson's and Henry's states of mind. McDilda became such an important person to the Japanese that he was brought to Tokyo for more briefings. That was where he was when the emperor formally announced Japan's surrender, and he survived the war. But more than fifty U.S. airmen in custody back in his prison were immediately beheaded by Japanese soldiers, as were many others following the emperor's announcement. Quincy and Henry saw that as clear confirmation that they were right to take the Hyena quickly to the shed and kill him—before he killed them.

The last time they had talked about their war experience was in a late-night phone call six months before. Henry had called Watson to tell him about a newspaper story he'd just

read describing how the whole country of Japan had gone
haywire because a twelve-year-old boy had beheaded an
eleven-year-old boy. "They're acting like it never happened
before in their lovely peaceful country," Henry said. "They
invented goddamn beheading!"

It was a jarring call, and Watson had told Henry to go
back to sleep. Forget the whole thing, he said. It was fifty
years ago.

"Sometimes, Quincy, when I close my eyes, it wasn't fifty
years ago," Henry had said.

"It's always for me," Watson had replied—and, at that
moment, truly believed.

He had long before stopped making references in sermons
to his prisoner experience and had deleted mention of it from
his introductions and bios. He didn't mind being known as a
command pilot of a B-29 bomber in World War II but he finally became weary of having Methodist congregations told
that he walked with a cane because of what happened to him
in a prisoner-of-war camp. He came—slowly, to be sure—to
the conclusion that he did not want forever to be the
preacher who had been tortured by the Japs.

The Sheraton waitress did not hold up her end of the deal.
As Henry and Watson finished their breakfast, a grinning fat
man in a white chef's uniform and tall hat appeared at their
table.

"I hope I not interrupt important something," said the
man in an accent that seemed vaguely European. So did his
round olive face with its wispy black mustache.

"We were talking about sex, specifically about getting the
bishop laid," Henry said, without missing a beat.

"Oh, my, no—I apologize, I so sorry," said the chef, the
olive in his face now tinted slightly red. "I came to say you
Very Reverend Bishop Watson are most famous great person ever I fix for and I hope you not gassed for killing that
man . . ."

He left before finishing his sentence.

Watson wanted to laugh at Henry's outrageous wit. And he wanted to whack him for it, too. These competing reactions had collided many times in their fifty-year friendship.

"That guy is going to tell some reporter that we were talking about sex," Watson said.

"Good if he does," Henry replied. "It'll help the image."

Watson's last conversation about sex had been with Joyce.

When she was in her mid sixties, her heart had begun to go bad from an inherited genetic weakness of the muscles. A bypass operation, a couple of angioplasties, and a series of different experimental medicines held off the inevitable for a while, but she was not physically able to even consider the only long-term solution, a transplant.

Watson was with her most every moment of the final three months of her life, including the last four days at Methodist Hospital in San Antonio. He asked for her final thoughts—she spoke openly about all these thoughts being final—about not having children or grandchildren to be with her as she died.

"We all have to make choices, Quincy my love," she said.

She asked that he stand up there close by her at the side of the bed. Then she smiled, reached over, and gave his crotch a velvet, loving pat.

"If they had not been damaged, you wouldn't have given me the time of day."

Watson quickly and strongly denied their lovely, awful truth for a final time.

"So, spell it out, Quincy," Henry said now. "What is it specifically that bothers you about getting under the sheets with the woman in the Italian restaurant?"

"Well, there are only a few things that can be done that . . . well, do the trick, so to speak."

"Such as?"

"Such as also I'm a Methodist minister. I can't go around

jumping in bed with just anybody. You know what I mean."

"Oh, right, Reverend. I forgot about your preacher shit. Look. See it as a God's-will kind of thing. God, in his wisdom, looked down and saw that one of his most devoted servants, the Very Most Reverend John Quincy Watson of San Antonio, had not had a satisfying experience with a woman since his wife died five years ago. So it came to pass that God—always thoughtful and sympathetic—went to his Rolodex and found a woman with the proper urge and beliefs. And he saith to her: 'Go ye, woman, into the land of linguini and mozzarella cheese and seek him out. Invite him to experience your most precious treasures. Seek out and perform whatever it takes to do the trick for and on him . . .' "

Watson started laughing so hard and so loud that soon almost everyone in the coffee shop turned to look. Some, no doubt, were wondering what in the world the Methodist bishop killer had to laugh about.

Then the sons appeared at the entrance, talking animatedly to each other. Had they been at it all night?

Henry quickly asked Watson, "How are you leaning? A deal or a trial?"

"A deal. And it's more than a lean. I want to go home and resume some kind of normal life."

"Good luck on that, Bishop Celebrity."

.   .   .

They began with a glass of a very cold champagne served by one of her Filipino house staff.

"I'm not sure I have ever born witness to a more magnificent sight," said the bishop with absolute sincerity.

They were on an elevated back veranda with a view of the Pacific and a bright blue-and-purple horizon in which his imagination had no problem projecting paradise somewhere.

It was almost nine o'clock at night, but it might as well have been nine in the morning. The sights were that visible and spectacular.

She said, "Dear me, sometimes you can find me out here for days on end, sitting, lying, eating, drinking, reading, and thinking, leaving only occasionally when I have to do something boring or necessary."

Watson had lied to Henry when he said he hadn't called the woman in the restaurant. It was what he considered a good lie—told in the furtherance of good rather than bad. The good in this case being that Henry, as close a friend as he was, had no reason to know about it.

She had sent a car and driver for him. The car was a huge dark blue Mercedes, the driver a small Filipino in a black uniform. They took him to this place, to her incredibly large and luxurious oceanside villa in nearby La Jolla.

Now, taking his eyes from the spectacular view to her, he realized with considerable alarm that he could not remember her name. He had her original note in his shirt pocket, but he couldn't take it out and look at it. Not at this moment with the champagne and the sky and the ocean.

Was it Jean? No, no. Rebecca? Yes, that was it. No! That must have been in his head from the TV series *Rebecca* he caught the other night on PBS. Rachel? Rosemary? Mary Lee? Teresa? Sue?

She was saying how she planned to be glued to her television when the trial started and how she thought the whole thing would make for absolutely breathtaking and moving television—more dramatic and important than either the O.J. or Menendez brothers trials.

"You will not only be acquitted, you will be sent out of that courtroom an American hero," she said. "They'll be playing band music for you, naming bridges and airports after you."

Watson said his lawyers weren't so sure of that. Henry junior had in fact already begun to harp on the point that their most effective defense might be to convince the jury that both Tashimotos really did deserve to die.

She continued: "Well, whatever. Most of us live our lives without ever having to confront the kind of things you did. I admire you so."

So, she may be perceptive as well as attractive, Watson thought. She really was a pretty woman, perhaps almost twenty years younger than him, well groomed and well presented. Her eyes, light green and now filling with tears, were as invitational as a flashing neon sign. As a bishop, he spent a fair amount of time dealing with the fallout from invitations women offered with their eyes and other means to Methodist ministers who, to their stunning surprise, discovered they were as susceptible as ordinary mortals to the attractions of illicit sex. It was particularly hard to resist if the woman was also offering you God status.

"Were you ever tempted to be an airline pilot or to fly airplanes of any kind after the war?" she asked.

No, he said. He had been a pilot for two and a half years for the U.S. Army Air Forces. It was an experience, not a life.

He did not tell her that his desire to be a pilot jumped out of his soul forever when he jumped out of that bomb-bay door over Japan. He did not tell her it was not unusual for pilots who lose planes never to fly one again. He did not tell her about Sandy Anderson of Cedar Rapids, Iowa, who, on his twenty-fourth bombing mission, brought his crippled B-29 back to Saipan with two engines out, one on fire and the fourth barely sputtering. The wheels wouldn't come down, so Sandy crash-landed on the plane's bare belly. He was one of only four of his eleven-man crew to survive, and he ran away from the burning plane sobbing like a baby. He refused to ever fly another plane—B-29 or anything else. He wouldn't

even ride in one as a passenger. Diagnosed by the flight sur-
geons as suffering from some kind of acute battle-fatigue dis-
order, he returned to the States on a troopship.

"I would think being a pilot would be exciting work," she
said.

"Not as exciting as being a preacher," he said.

"I hate what those Japanese did to you," she said. "The
Japanese I know around here seem so gentle and kind . . .
what should I call you? 'Bishop' or 'Reverend' doesn't quite
fit the occasion, I don't think."

"Quincy is fine with me," he said.

"Then we'll be first names all the way. Good."

That rather precluded his asking something like, And
what should I call *you*, ma'am?

"We're both grown-ups," she said after their glasses had
been discreetly refilled. Watson had also eaten a few bites of
thin, exquisite salmon on a piece of delicately cut brown
bread. "Would you like to have dinner before or after?"

Before or after *what*? he asked himself and then almost
immediately answered.

"What are we having?" Watson asked her.

She gave out a hoot of laughter that got him laughing, too.

Soon they were in her bedroom, which seemed larger than
most Methodist sanctuaries. The four-poster king-sized bed
appeared small there in the center of the room, which was
decorated mostly in off-whites, illuminated with soft lights,
and now filled with CD music of soothing violins.

They kissed and caressed standing up, and then they sat
down on the edge of the bed. He had already taken off his
blue blazer. She unbuttoned his open-neck blue-and-white
checked sport shirt and pulled it out from his tan gabardine
slacks. He removed his oxblood penny loafers.

"Now," she said, "maybe we should talk some technique
here before proceeding further. Do you agree, Quincy?"

Watson agreed.

"But while we talk, let's remove the pants, okay?"

"No, not the pants. Not yet."

"You've got something in mind that we can do with your pants on, Quincy?"

He told her that he was very sensitive about showing his terribly scarred right leg. He suggested they take it gradually and let the passion of the moment help remove some of his reluctance and eventually his trousers.

"Fine," she said. "But once we get the pants off, what is it that I can do to give you full pleasure and satisfaction?"

He told her.

"That sounds a bit on the peculiar side," she said, "but if that works for you, then that is what it shall be."

They continued to do little things aimed at arriving at a suitable moment of passion. Most involved removing her clothing, which was a relatively simple operation. She was wearing a multicolored hostess gown that buttoned—and, obviously, unbuttoned—down the front. There was nothing much underneath.

"All right," said the bishop. "I'm ready for my pants to come off now."

"Hallelujah!" she exclaimed. It was a biblical term he would have just as soon she had not mentioned. But, it's not possible to control everything.

Then she carefully removed two exquisite gold earrings and a matching bracelet and placed them on the bedside table. "Bill always reminds me to take off the jewelry—it could get lost in all the commotion."

"Bill?" he said, as she unbuckled his belt and unzipped his fly.

"My husband."

"You're married?"

"Isn't everybody? But not to worry. He's in Bangkok on business—be back over the weekend."

John Quincy Watson, the retired Methodist bishop of San Antonio, was back in the car on his way to his hotel in less than two minutes.

Her name was Susan, according to her original note, which he took out of his pocket and read.

He never did find out what was for dinner.

CHAPTER SEVENTEEN

They were at the Sheraton pool. Henry sat in a beach chair under a blue-and-white striped umbrella reading a Robert Parker detective novel set in Boston. Watson had taken a break from reading through the stack of letters that he brought outside. Hundreds of them had arrived at the hotel, offering him everything from full support or absolute condemnation to invitations to be interviewed on the Internet as well as on radio and television and at luncheons and dinners and to preach at churches in San Diego and all over the world.

He was in the pool, doing laps again. Watson did a lot of laps because he believed his daily swimming was one of the many things that had helped bring his leg and most of the rest of him back to life and kept him that way all of these years. The especially mild and warm weather of San Antonio and his insistence on the perk of a swimming pool at the bishop's residence had made the daily difference. There was also a pool now at the smaller new ranch-style home he'd bought in a San Antonio suburb when he retired.

Now the sons strolled toward the pool from the hotel lobby. Henry junior was returning from a meeting with the San Diego district attorney; Doug Wilson, most likely, had simply followed Henry junior there and back. Henry junior was frowning; Doug was smiling.

Henry junior said of the district attorney: "The bastard won't budge from a plea to second-degree murder. He says it was too premeditated for voluntary manslaughter. Second-degree means twenty-five years, possibly trimmed back some with a recommendation of mercy."

"Twenty-five years?" said Watson, out of the pool now and dripping wet. "Where?"

"In some California prison, I'm sorry to say, Bishop."

"I'll be almost a hundred years old by then . . ."

"The guy's nuts," Henry senior said. "He couldn't get a jury of *Japs* to return that kind of sentence on these facts."

"I know, I know, Dad. I told him that in very direct and certain terms. He said, Feel free to test the courage of your beliefs before a judge and jury, Counselor. He's lined up airline attendants and agents and a hotel clerk and others from that day to make the case for the bishop having stalked the victim with the preset determination to murder him. It won't sell, but that's the prosecution's spin. By the way, Dad, watch the Japs comments until we get this case behind us, okay?"

"Okay," his father said. "What's going on here?"

"This Jim Radcliff—he's the D.A.—wants a trial, that's what's going on. He sees how big this thing has become. Methodist bishop tries to settle old World War II score against Japanese. As we have all seen, it's great copy, great cable-TV programming. He's read all those newspaper and magazine stories, and now he sees all those TV cameras outside this hotel and down at the courthouse—God, are those people persistent and obnoxious—and he sees himself as the new governor of California or, if he really scores, as the new Marcia Clark."

"Marcia Clark? She lost an open-and-shut case! O.J.'s on the golf course instead of fried meat because of her!"

"None of that win-lose stuff matters anymore, you know that, Dad. She became a star."

The father, the lawyer, said nothing in response to his son, the lawyer. Then they settled down to decide there was really nothing to decide.

There would be a trial.

.   .   .

Four weeks later, St. Luke's of San Diego, like Susan of La Jolla, sent a car and driver to pick Watson up. The driver was a young off-duty fire captain who was a member of the church. He used back roads to bring the black Lincoln town car, rock star–style, to an obscure back door of the main church building.

They had promised Bishop Watson a large and friendly congregation of worshippers and to keep away the press and other celebrity hunters and curiosity seekers. The invitation stressed that they were interested in him as a sensational preacher, not as the defendant in a sensational murder case.

Henry Howell, Jr., always his father's son, had threatened to resign from the case if Bishop Watson went ahead with his plans to preach this morning at St. Luke's, San Diego's largest and most prestigious Methodist church. He did so during a walk he demanded his father and Watson take with him along the San Diego waterfront by the many hotels and restaurants.

"You remember what the San Diego cops said when they came to your hotel room that evening of the death, Bishop?" he had said.

"They read me my rights and warnings."

"Correct, sir. And let me give you another warning: Everything you say from that pulpit tomorrow morning can and will be used against you in a court of law. Don't do it, please. Not on the day before the trial begins."

Watson, wearing sunglasses in order to avoid being recognized, had argued that when he stepped into that pulpit he would do so as John Quincy Watson, ordained minister of the United Methodist Church, not as John Quincy Watson, criminal defendant.

"Wrong, sir. I'm sorry, but you are both and one in the same, and never the twain can be parted. I would remind you that the judge has allowed you to be free on bond since the night of your arrest. That is most unusual in any murder case, much less a high-visibility one like yours. He did so because you were such a distinguished clergyman, somebody who, though accused of murder, was otherwise trustworthy and an all-around good human being—somebody who would show up for trial and not run to Brazil or wherever."

"I would never go to Brazil," Watson had said, glancing first at Henry senior and then across at a large gray navy warship at a shipyard across the harbor.

"Right, the South of France, maybe," Henry senior had chimed in. "Tuscany, for sure, and certainly a beach in Thailand—but Brazil, no."

"This is not funny, Dad!"

Henry junior had shown his disgust with a dramatic upward thrust of his hands and shoulders, then he'd huffed and stormed away.

Henry senior had said to Watson, "Don't worry about him. He's not quitting. But the boy's right, Quincy. Whatever you say in that sermon is going to be all over television and the press. The prosecution and maybe even prospective jurors will be listening to every word. It's a risky business. Do you really have to do it?"

Watson had said he really did.

Now he was greeted by Michael Clement, the senior minister of St. Luke's. Watson liked preachers. Sure, there were fools and losers in the Methodist ministry just like in other denominations and other lines of work. Watson had come across political operators, backstabbers, thieves, and adulterers, and, worst of all, the holier-than-thous who acted as if they really were God on earth. But mostly, to Watson's experience, Methodist ministers were good, well-meaning men and women who tried their very best to do the right things for the right reasons. And like Michael Clement, his host this Sunday morning, most were friendly, gregarious, and easy to be with. The best ones were also terrific storytellers as well as being emotional, passionate, hyper. The intellectual quiet types, those who came to the ministry slowly through reading and study, could be good, but seldom were they great.

"How did you happen to come into the ministry?" Clement asked as they went to his office for robing.

It's a good question for a fellow preacher to ask, Watson thought. It tells so much about you.

.   .   .

It had happened in Austin after a panel discussion before two hundred or so members of the Methodist student group at the University of Texas.

Watson and Joyce had chosen U.T. for him to finish college because it was close to San Antonio, where he would have to return often as an outpatient. Also, because he became a Texas resident, he could go there for almost nothing, which, with the added help of the G.I. Bill, meant no financial strains. U.T. accepted all of his Amherst credits and put him on a special fast track for veterans that made it possible to earn a bachelor's degree in business administration in eighteen months.

The discussion that night was about the Christian morality of the bombing of Hiroshima and Nagasaki. Watson was on the panel in his capacity as an active Methodist, a decorated World War II B-29 pilot, and a surviving Japanese prisoner of war. There were three other lay Methodists on the panel—a right-winger from Dallas and two strong antibomb moralists from the U.T. faculty.

They caused Watson to lose his temper.

One of the antibomb professors—he had been a War Department historian or something else nonmilitary during the war—said, "These American pilots who dropped those bombs are as much war criminals as Tōjō or any of the other Japanese who've been tried and executed."

"War criminals?" Watson bellowed. "Are you out of your goddamn mind? That's what the Japs called all of us who flew B-29s!"

The professor, a wiry man in glasses, suggested Watson calm down his spirit and his language. "You were correctly called war criminals, I would say—*all* of you."

"The Japs started the war, you idiot!"

The professor replied, "I don't have to listen to this god-less right-wing militaristic nationalism."

Watson responded, "In the name of God and truth, it was either them or us! I was in a prison camp. If those bombs hadn't been dropped, the war would have gone on and on until the last Japanese and millions of Americans—including, most assuredly, me—were dead. More Japanese civilians had already died in the firebombings of Tokyo and other cities than at either Hiroshima or Nagasaki. But they wouldn't quit. Not until the big bombs came down."

"How many innocent Japanese civilians did you person-ally kill with *your* bombs, Mr. Watson?"

"I don't know."

"What kind of bombs did you drop?"

"Incendiary and other kinds . . ."

"Firebombs? The kind that burned people and their homes to crisps? Oh, yes. A few hundred thousand more of their innocent women and children had to be incinerated

with atomic bombs so you and a few more of our combat-
ants could live? That's abhorrently racist as well as anti-
Christian and anti-Methodist. Kill the little yellow people so
we big white people can live. God bless America."

"You fool! You stupid, goddamn fool!"

"Can't you say anything without getting personal and
profane?"

"This *is* personal and profane!"

"You need help, Watson. Go see a shrink or a preacher of
your choice, and come back when you're feeling civilized."

The wiry professor didn't realize how close he came to not
getting out of the student-union building alive. Watson's
rage was such that he could easily have beheaded him,
kicked his brains out, or clubbed him with his cane. The hate
and anger that Watson thought had passed on through him
with Rick's help hadn't gone anywhere after all.

Joyce, from her seat in the front row, took charge. She
stood up and got Watson out of there.

"You should be ashamed!" some woman yelled at Watson
as they left the room.

"Killer pilot!" screamed a young man.

Joyce led Watson, like he was a mad dog—or a Japanese
special prisoner—on a short leash, outside and off campus to
a small dark bar in a shopping strip called the Drag.

They had a few beers and many words.

Yes, Watson shared the horror at the destruction his B-29
colleagues showered on those Japanese people of Hiroshima
and Nagasaki. But, really truly, if those bombs had not been
dropped, he would be dead. It was only a matter of weeks—
maybe days—before his usefulness as a redheaded karate
dummy would have been over. The Hyena would have either
chopped off his head or, more likely, stood him up in front
of the prisoner formation and simply kicked him to death.
Watson saw that as a matter of reality and survival, not of
nuke politics or morality or religion.

The two hours or so in that bar did not end with his deciding to be a Methodist minister instead of a businessman. But that was when he started seriously thinking about it. Why? What was the connection between his fit that night and being a preacher? He didn't really know.

He was already a real Methodist. By the time he was discharged from Brooke as an outpatient, he and Joyce were fully hooked, having become active members of the Fort Sam Houston Methodist Church in San Antonio and its adult Sunday school. That was Rick Allison's doing. In helping Watson through the nightmares and hate crises, he had turned him into a Christian.

Their relationship continued through Watson's frequent trips to the hospital and even after Rick was discharged from the army and returned to parish life in Alamogordo. The two talked often about religion and church, as well as those many other little subjects such as the meaning and purpose of life. Some of their most ferocious conversations were about an Almighty God that would permit the wanton killing and abuse of His American children by His Japanese children, and vice versa.

Rick engaged on this. He understood, especially after returning home and discovering that New Mexico had had a huge number of men in Japanese prison camps, particularly because a New Mexico National Guard antiaircraft unit, activated for special duty before the war, had been at Bataan. Only four hundred—less than half of them—came home alive. Later, monuments to particular men would spring up in small towns throughout the state.

Watson rode a bus out to Alamogordo to discuss with Rick going to a seminary instead of a Wall Street brokerage firm or a large corporation. Six months had passed since Watson's blowup at the Methodist student meeting.

"You're not thinking you can hide from your anger under a black robe, are you, Quincy?" he asked. Always Rick.

"No," Watson sighed. "I think that's where I can . . . well, you know, feel good about myself by helping other people feel good about themselves by believing in and doing the Lord's work."

"Why?"

"Because, because, because. As a minister I can deal with other people's problems and maybe . . . well, pay back some dues for having survived."

Rick said, "God chose you to live, and so now you must do good?"

"Something like that, sure."

"Forget it. The ministry's not a form of therapy, Quincy. It's a commitment, a belief, a way of life."

And then, after annoying Watson that way for a while he hugged him and said he couldn't be happier that his friend had chosen to be a minister of the Lord. He later wrote a letter and made a few phone calls to help Watson get accepted at the Perkins School of Theology, a part of Southern Methodist University and his own alma mater, in Dallas.

"This is a man with special life experiences that make him uniquely qualified to help others grapple with the dilemmas of faith and conscience," Rick wrote. "He will be a truly great preacher."

.   .   .

Now in San Diego, as he stepped into a black robe, Watson answered the minister's question by saying, "It mostly had to do with my experiences in World War II."

Reverend Clement was almost as tall as Watson and about twenty years younger. He was clearly nervous and excited to be in Watson's private presence. "We're all praying and pulling for you tomorrow, Bishop," he said just before they walked down a flight of stairs and a long hallway to the sanctuary.

"Then it's too bad you can't be on the jury," said Watson, keeping it light. "In fact, I think you'd make a great foreman."

He followed Clement out through a door to the side of the huge pipe organ into the sanctuary. The choir, a terrific one, was singing "Bringing in the Sheaves." He and Clement came to a stop and remained standing in front of two ornate wooden chairs behind the rostrum on the pulpit platform. The music continued.

The place was packed. Every pew was filled, as were many folding chairs that had been placed in the aisles and in the front and rear to handle the spillover. Watson was an experienced congregation counter. He smiled his best preacher's smile as he moved his head to make eye contact with the entire congregation. Fifteen hundred was his crowd estimate. Not a bad house, José, he said to himself, using a line from a bad sixties TV show that he and Joyce had adopted as their private way to refer to the Sunday-morning multitudes. Fifteen hundred San Diegoans all eager to hear what the bishop of San Antonio/murderer of a Japanese businessman had to say.

They had to wait a few standard order-of-worship minutes for the main event. Clement offered a brief invocation about the glory of God and this day in San Diego. Then the congregation sang "A Mighty Fortress Is Our God." Clement read from the Book of Mark about resolving conflict, and the choir sang again—"Onward, Christian Soldiers"— as ushers wearing white gardenia boutonnieres passed collection plates.

Clement then introduced Bishop Watson as "a war hero, a man of God, a man who, while facing a severe personal crisis, comes to us this Sunday morning to do what he does best—preach the Word of the Lord."

Watson stood, closed his eyes, bowed his head in a quick

silent prayer, and walked, as always with the help of his cane, to the pulpit.

He was comfortable here. This was his place. This was something he did well—better than most. He had discovered his talent early on, during his first classes on preaching technique—the subject is called homiletics—at Perkins. How many sermons had he delivered since in his forty-three years as a Methodist minister? Two thousand? Three thousand? A million?

Until now, he had considered the most important sermon of his life to be the one he delivered to nineteen people at a small Methodist church in Comfort, Texas, on June 4, 1953. That church in the summer-camp hill country north of San Antonio was his first assignment after his ordination. He and Joyce had developed a special affection for San Antonio, so it was to that Methodist district that he applied and was accepted. Joyce had put the typed manuscript of the Comfort sermon into a scrapbook of photographs, church bulletins, and other memorabilia of his pastorates from Comfort on through Stockdale, Seguin, Uvalde, Harlingen, Victoria, Corpus Christi, and, finally, San Antonio itself, as the senior minister of the downtown First Methodist Church. He was elected bishop for the San Antonio District in 1978 and served in that position until his retirement.

Now came *this* sermon—another one for the scrapbook, he thought. Maybe as the last sermon he ever delivered?

He thanked Reverend Clement, praised the choir and the music, and extended his best wishes and good morning to the people of St. Luke's. Then he spoke for several minutes about the need for everyone to be charitable toward those with differing points of view on everything from philosophy and religion to sports and politics. He said, among other things, that it was important to remember that wisdom included knowing when to listen as well as when to speak about what you knew or thought. Knowing what you don't know is more important than knowing what you do, he told them.

Then, after a brief pause and a smiling survey of the faces in front of him, he did what they had really come to hear him do. Speaking in his firm, quiet voice, he said, " 'Thou shall not kill,' said the Lord. And yet, I have killed. There are forces still in me that I had thought were long gone. I do not have the control over myself that I believed—and took for granted—that my Christian faith and good common sense had given me. I had not realized how deeply the seeds of hate and violence were planted in me by an experience of war over fifty years ago.

"There really is the Devil in us all. One would think I would have been an exception. No Devil in me—a retired bishop of the Methodist church, a man who gave himself to the ministry and to God as an ordained minister more than forty years ago. But I do not say to you, and let no other man or woman ever say, 'the Devil made me do it.' The Devil is in us all, but he is never in charge, he never makes us do anything. It is the power to say yes, no, maybe so that distinguishes us from all other forms of life. We are the ones with the minds and the moral compasses. We are always in charge. We are thinking souls, responsible for our own actions, our own destinies, our own happiness.

"That is what I have always believed and preached from pulpits like this all of my adult life. But what I discovered on a recent evening here in your wonderful city of San Diego was that I could not practice what I preached.

"I have prayed to God for forgiveness for what I have done. I hereby, in your company and in your house of worship, ask your forgiveness and that of Methodists and Christians and good people everywhere. I mostly seek the forgiveness of the wife and children and others who loved the man who died.

"I can only hope that someday they and you and everyone

else can find it in their hearts to forgive me. Forgiving is not easy, as I know from my own experience.

"At the Bay Heights Methodist Church in Corpus Christi, Texas, on March 12, 1967, twenty years after the end of World War II, I said the following to a congregation of folks just like you: 'My experience as a prisoner of war has brought home to me in a powerful and lasting way what the Christian concept of forgiveness means. It has been difficult and painful, but I stand before you this Sunday morning without hate or loathing for those who imprisoned or hurt me. I hold this cane up as a symbol of that forgiveness, not of pain and suffering. The ability to forgive is one of the most important gifts God has given us. It makes it possible always to move from the dark spots and moments of life to light ones.' End quote.

"Again, I have failed to live up to my words. But that does not invalidate them. They are as true today as they were the day I first preached them more than thirty years ago.

"As the old saying goes, I beseech you to do as I say, not as I do."

The congregation gave him a resounding standing ovation of applause and amens.

They said on television that night and in the newspapers the next morning that nothing like that had ever happened before at a mainline Protestant church in San Diego—or possibly anywhere else in California.

CHAPTER EIGHTEEN

The trial judge, superior-court justice Amanda Haynes Lawton, had warned everyone about not turning this into another California courtroom circus. She put a gag order on the lawyers, kept the jurors anonymous and sequestered, and from the beginning made it clear that no showboating or unnecessary delay would be tolerated. A rigid no-reentry policy was set for the press and the few members of the public who would be allowed in the courtroom each day. Nobody could enter or leave the courtroom except during breaks in the trial.

But she did permit live television coverage, which led Court TV and two of the three national cable-news networks to go gavel-to-gavel. The commercial networks and various other cable talk shows also rounded up the usual-suspect defense lawyers and former prosecutors for analysis to go with their fulsome excerpts coverage.

District attorney Radcliff, a rangy six-footer who had been a star quarterback at UCLA, moved and spoke from the beginning with an air of confidence. And from his opening statement onward, he left no doubt as to where the prosecution was going.

He told the jury, "The defense, with the help of the national news media and even some well-meaning people with legitimate grievances from the past, have attempted to turn this case into a struggle about history and war crimes. It is nothing of the kind, ladies and gentlemen. It is about a cold-blooded murder of one human being by another."

He scoffed at the idea that the killing was self-defense, pointing to Bishop Watson at the counsel table and asking, "An unarmed man standing five feet five inches high and weighing less than one hundred thirty pounds is a threat to that man? Please! Bishop John Quincy Watson, as I am sure you have already observed, is a man of some height and heft."

He also knocked down justifiable homicide as a possible defense. Even if Bishop Watson honestly believed the victim was the man who had harmed him fifty years ago in a World War II prisoner-of-war camp, it did not justify murder. "A democratic, civilized society does not settle those scores privately one-on-one, *mano a mano*. We have courts for doing that."

Apologizing in advance for evidence that would be graphic and gruesome, Radcliff said the state of California would prove beyond a reasonable doubt that the defendant stalked and then murdered the victim, using a second method when the first didn't do the trick. The nature and method of the crime, he said, more than warranted a finding of guilty to the charge of second-degree murder.

"In the unreal world of television and movie drama they talk a lot about open-and-shut cases," Radcliff continued. "Well, here, finally, life is imitating art. There has never been a more open-and-shut case than the one you are about to decide."

Henry Howell, Jr., in a brief opening statement for the defense, disputed two of Radcliff's points. Yes, ladies and gentlemen, this was self-defense and it was justified. He also emphasized that Bishop Watson was not denying having killed Bill Joe Tashimoto. "What you must decide," he said, "is why he did it, and whether that constitutes grounds for acquittal under the laws of California. I have no doubt that you will decide easily, unanimously, and quickly that as a matter of law and conscience, the Reverend John Quincy Watson deserves to walk out of this courtroom a free man."

He ended by also apologizing in advance for some evidence that the defense would be presenting. "To understand *this* trial of the Reverend John Quincy Watson it is crucial that you first understand his earlier trials at the hands of the Japanese."

Then Radcliff and his team got right to the stalk. In quick, chronological order, the American Airlines attendant and counter agents at the DFW and San Diego airports testified about their brief encounters with Watson. So did the room clerk at the Hotel Bayfront. Despite security and privacy policy to the contrary, she said, she felt at ease giving the information to the tall, distinguished-looking elderly man with the cane because of the small silver cross he wore in his lapel. She assumed he was a minister because her own minister wore one.

Howell, on cross-examination, asked all of these witnesses the same three questions.

"Did the bishop say to you, 'I want to find that man Tashimoto so I can kill him?'

"'So I can break his neck?'

"'So I can toss him off a hotel balcony?'"

To each question, every witness answered no.

The next witnesses were a San Diego Police homicide detective and the San Diego County medical examiner. The detective was among those officers who came to the Hotel Bayfront suite after Watson's phone call. He did the official arresting and reading of rights, and took a written statement later at police headquarters.

Radcliff brought on the examiner, Dr. Ralph Mueller, mostly for the purpose of introducing some photographs and making one major point—that Tashimoto was not dead when he was thrown over the balcony. "It was the impact of his body on the concrete patio that caused death," Mueller explained to the hushed courtroom. "He died almost instantly from the crash and multiple fractures to his entire body, internally as well as externally."

"Absolutely no question that Mr. Tashimoto was still very much alive when he hit the concrete?"

"That's right."

Radcliff looked down at some papers on the counsel's table, letting that answer and its triggered image linger with the jury for a few seconds.

Then, his voice lowered, he asked how much the victim weighed.

One hundred and twenty-nine and three-quarters pounds, Mueller replied.

"How would you describe his physique, his build?"

"Slight."

"He was tiny for a man?"

"By American standards, yes, sir."

That's when Radcliff brought out the photographs of Bill Joe Tashimoto's crushed and mangled body. Some were taken at the death scene on the hotel patio, others on an autopsy table at the morgue. Some were in black-and-white, others in bright, vivid colors.

A principal preoccupation of the reporters and others in court and in the television audience was to observe Bishop Watson's every reaction, no matter how slight or minute, to what was happening in the courtroom.

This time, it was plain for all to see.

One of the defense lawyers, sitting on Watson's left at the counsel table, was looking through the photographs in preparation for their being offered officially into evidence and then shown to the jury.

Watson grabbed the photos from the man, looked at two

or three of them, then turned them over and slapped them down hard on the table.

Then he closed his eyes, bowed his head, and visibly shook as if weeping or gagging.

Oh, dear God, why did you let Rick go? I need him so right now—right this very minute.

.   .   .

The call from Rick Allison had come at ten o'clock at night, about a year and a half ago.

"I'm calling to say so long, Quincy," he said. "And to give you a few assignments—if, as they say on *Mission: Impossible,* you choose to accept them."

Watson knew that Rick and Judy had just returned from Houston. And he knew the situation. Rick had been told that his life would soon be over. Doctors in New Mexico, then in San Antonio at the University of Texas Medical School, where Watson got him to go, and, finally, at the M. D. Anderson Hospital and Tumor Institute in Houston had told him the same thing. There was a tumor growing up through the center of his body from his intestines that had metastasized beyond all possibilities for surgery, chemotherapy, or radiation. He had already begun to have steady pain, to lose weight, and to feel nauseated much of the time.

"I have made all of the major decisions about how I lived; I will now make them about the way I die. I will not lie up in a bed with tubes and prayers while Judy and the kids and you and my other friends cry and worry and speak softly. I'm seventy-eight years old, I've had a terrific life for myself and for the Lord, and I'm out of here."

Watson argued that it wasn't his decision. It is God who gives and God takes away.

"In theory, I agree with you—or at least I used to. But like many theories, in practice it sucks. God would not want me to suffer any more than I already have. He would not want the people who love me to suffer. So, please, Quincy. I have thought this through, and there is no talking me out of it."

"Where's Judy?"

"She's at Martha and Bill's baby-sitting the grandkids while they're out campaigning somewhere." Martha was their daughter; Bill, her husband, was a member of the New Mexico legislature. "Don't even think about calling over there. I'll be dead by the time they could get here anyhow."

Watson had had some experiences with suicidal people; it was part of being a minister. He had even taken a special course many years ago that a suicide-prevention psychologist had given in Dallas. He was now up against such an expert. Talking to potential suicides had been one of Rick's major specialties at Brooke after the war.

Talk, talk, talk was the main prevention tool; keep the person talking. The more time that goes by, the better the chance of a change of heart and mind. Most suicides are committed on emotional impulse. Talk, talk, talk until the moment passes.

Watson asked him how he planned to kill himself.

"That's not important," he said.

"Yeah, it is. Try not to make a mess. Think of Judy and the kids—the grandkids in particular—walking in and seeing you splattered all over the house. Is that fair to them?"

"Hey, Quincy, I know what you're up to. Keep the guy talking so it'll all go away. Forget it, friend. This is not going away any more than that tumor is. Okay?"

Okay.

"Now, here's what I want you to know. I've written a long note to Judy, and in it I have laid out what I want for a funeral—the music, the Scriptures, everything. I want you to do the eulogy and to preside. Will you do it?"

Funerals were the only part of Watson's work that he didn't handle particularly well. He could mouth the words of comfort and consolation, but he couldn't mean them. He sometimes thought that not being able to accept or be comfortable with death, in fact, may have been the most severe penalty he paid for those months as a prisoner. He couldn't participate at all in Joyce's funeral. More than a thousand people came to the First Methodist in downtown San Antonio, their old church. Rick presided. Watson spent most of the fifty-minute service sitting there in the front row with Henry and other friends, sobbing like a baby.

He would sob for Rick, but he would also preside.

Rick said, "I want you to talk about my decision to go my own way in accordance with my own schedule. Do not sweep it under the rug, Quincy."

"Forget it."

"Listen to me! This is an important issue, and I want it out there on the table."

Watson said he was not about to preach about the goodness and mercy of suicide for him or anyone else.

"Listen to me!" Rick yelled. "It isn't your sermon. It's mine. Use my actions, my words to get it there. Tell them that you talked to me tonight, tell them that I was determined to do it on my own terms because I believe this is the way it should be."

Watson said nothing. He heard Rick taking a breath, settling down.

Rick, his voice almost back to normal, then said, almost as if he had rehearsed it, "I believe dying should not have to be an act of humiliation and degradation. I don't want Judy or anybody else to feed me mashed potatoes with a spoon or wipe my ass after removing the bedpan. I don't want an army of doctors and nurses wasting their valuable time and resources on me. I do not want to wither away as a vegetable, a living, senile, brainless corpse. Do you, Quincy? How does that sound to *you* as a way to go?"

"This conversation is not about my death, Rick. It's about yours."

"Fine, fine. This *is* my decision about mine. In the name of God the Father and the Son and the Holy Ghost, I believe in what I am doing. I believe it more strongly than anything I have ever believed except my belief in God the Father and the Son and the Holy Ghost, Quincy."

"Taking one's life is not a belief, Rick."

"Don't preach to me, Quincy! In the name of God, listen to me!"

"All right, all right. I'm listening."

"I want you to say what I believe at the funeral. Will you do it?"

"I'm not sure I can. It goes against everything both of us preached, for one thing."

"Well, maybe what we've been preaching is wrong."

Watson stayed with him on the issue—talking, talking, talking—for as long as he could before Rick finally shut him up and forced an answer. Will you talk about it at my funeral? Will you accurately report my beliefs to my mourners?

Watson promised he would.

Then he tried to engage Rick in an argument over the act of suicide. How could you do what you prevented so many others from doing? Taking one's own life, no matter the reason, is a sin and an unforgivable one. Rick rejected everything Watson said. "Suicide to avoid one's debts or humiliation or jail or a bad marriage or job or something like that is not a good or permissible or forgivable thing to do. What I am doing is in another whole and special category reserved only for the terminally and hopelessly ill. Period."

Then, quite suddenly, he said, "Good-bye, Quincy. You've been a great friend, and I will miss you dearly. See you in the Kingdom of Heaven."

He was gone before Watson could respond.

Watson immediately dialed the police in Alamogordo. By the time they got to his house, Rick was already dead. He had hung himself with a rope, which he threw over an exposed rafter in the garage. The police said it was clear he had been talking to Watson from the garage on a portable phone.

Watson kept his word. There were a lot of Methodist preachers at the funeral who clearly were not comfortable hearing a retired bishop talking from a pulpit about one of their own who had believed in the right of terminally and hopelessly sick people to die with dignity—by their own hand.

What Rick's death meant right now, sitting in this San Diego courtroom, was that Watson was now down to one. First he lost Joyce, then Rick. Of the three people who'd brought him back from Sengei 4, only Henry remained.

It was Rick he needed to help him move on now from these awful photos of Bill Joe Tashimoto's crushed, bleeding, mangled, grotesque little body. Just thinking of Rick, a man of such enormous moral strength, gave Watson a quick shot of hope about his own ability to cope one more time, to move on again.

The feeling lasted only until he realized that these photos, like Rick's tumor, would never go away.

.   .   .

The prosecution rested its case after a day they had designated for telling the life story of Bill Joe Tashimoto. The witness was Mrs. Satchiko Tashimoto, the victim's widow, who was also the director of the New Nippon English-Speaking Society. Radcliff had brought her back from Tokyo to testify.

Mrs. Tashimoto was a small, attractive woman who exuded confidence and composure when she walked into the courtroom and took her seat in the witness chair. Although she had to be in her early seventies, her well-tailored light green suit and meticulously cared-for face and hair made her appear, to American eyes at least, to be in her early fifties.

Radcliff began by asking her to describe her husband in the most general of terms. She said, "My husband, may he rest in peace in Heaven, was a studious, calm, restrained, respectful, conscientious, hardworking, dignified human being. He was a man of honor and ideals, of principles and concepts. He was at peace with himself and with all others in his life."

Radcliff asked if, to her knowledge or witness, he had ever committed an act of violence against another person.

"Certainly not," she replied. "It is an unthinkable projection."

This was a woman who had come to San Diego with a very definite message to deliver, and she delivered it in a controlled, forceful, and precise manner in a deep, almost contralto voice that seemed larger than her body.

Why was her English so good? Radcliff asked.

"I am a teacher of the English language, as was my mother before me. My father was a professor of English literature in Tokyo and later in Kyoto. It is more than a second language to me. It is as familiar to me as my own language. Through my work, I continue to study and speak it and help others learn to do so."

She said she had met her husband in 1939 while both were students in her mother's English class in Tokyo. Her husband, one of the best students in the class, wanted to be a doctor of medicine, and he believed he would find the best medical education in the United States or Britain. He felt his education in either country would be much enhanced if he could speak good English.

"Why didn't he become a doctor?" asked Radcliff.

"The war came, and he was conscripted into the army. When he finally came out he thought it was too late to pursue a long, rigorous course of medical studies."

She described him as a man successful not only in the financial world but also in his personal life, as a husband to her, a father to their two sons and one daughter, and a grandparent of five.

"Did he talk to you about his life in the army during the war?" Radcliff asked.

"No. He told me that he was in Singapore, but he said it was an experience he wished to forget. He said there never should have been a war and that it had resulted in the deaths of millions of innocent people."

Was he proud of his service in the Japanese army?

"I never heard him use that term, *proud*, but he was certainly not ashamed. He saw it as his duty to the emperor."

How did he view Americans?

"He very much liked and appreciated Americans. With his knowledge of the English language, he was trained by the bank to specialize in dealing with American accounts. He spent much time with Americans and seemed to enjoy that time. He was not pleased about what the Americans did to our cities during the war. He was most upset at their use of huge bombs and worried so much throughout the war that the children and I might be killed or injured. But when the war was over he said all of our hostile thoughts toward the Americans, the British, the Chinese, and others must be over, too."

Mrs. Tashimoto brought the first real smiles to those in the courtroom when she recounted the story of how her husband came to be named Bill Joe. She said a family of Baptist missionaries from Indiana had come to his family's Tokyo neighborhood in the 1920s and converted almost every Japanese in sight and hearing to Christianity.

"His mother and father took the names of the two head male missionaries and gave them to their son. It was a source of embarrassment for my husband sometimes because his friends joked that it made him sound as if he were a singer of American songs that were called hillbilly."

The smiles disappeared during Henry junior's cross-examination and never returned.

Right off the bat, he handed her a photograph and asked if the young man in the uniform of a lieutenant in the Imperial Army of Japan was her husband. She said it was.

"What is that strapped to his right hip, Mrs. Tashimoto?" Henry junior asked.

"It appears to be a sword."

"Did he ever tell you what he did with that sword in Singapore?"

"No, no. He never talked about his war experiences."

"He did not say that he used it to behead Allied and other prisoners of war?"

Over Radcliff's overruled objection, Howell went for another direct hit.

"Mrs. Tashimoto, did your husband ever tell you what his duties were for the Japanese army in Singapore?"

"No. I have already said more than once that he did not tell me anything about the war."

"He did not say that his interest in being a doctor was at least satisfied by participation in random, atrocious, inhuman experiments on prisoners of war?"

Judge Lawton stopped Henry junior there.

But he had somewhere else to go. He asked if her husband was an expert in the martial arts. Yes, she said, he had been a black belt in karate at one time, but he had stopped participating in the sport.

"Why did he stop?"

Those watching for signs of nervousness and unease in the defendant, lawyers, and witnesses saw the first ones in Mrs. Tashimoto. She bit her lip and looked down in her lap before answering.

"I do not know, really. One day he simply told me he was no longer going to train or participate."

"Was there an incident of some kind, Mrs. Tashimoto?"

"Not that I recall."

Henry junior handed Mrs. Tashimoto a newspaper article and asked that it be marked as an exhibit for the defense. It was from the September 5, 1972, edition of the *Tokyo Shimbun,* one of Japan's largest dailies.

He asked her to translate and read it out loud for the judge and jury.

She read: " 'A forty-five-year-old attorney was seriously injured today in a karate accident. Police authorities identified the victim as Hori Sugawasi, who practices law with a large firm. He suffered severe brain damage after being kicked in the head by one of his karate associates, who was identified as Bill Joe Tashimoto, a businessman of Tokyo.' "

Henry junior asked, "Did the injured lawyer recover, or was his brain permanently damaged?"

She said she didn't know.

"How does that incident square with your testimony about your husband being such a peaceful man?"

"In Japan, Mr. Howell, the martial arts are considered the sport of peaceful men."

Henry junior wasn't finished. He asked, "Are you aware of the atrocities Japanese soldiers committed against American pilots and other airmen during World War II?"

Only vaguely, she said.

"Have you read a book about the B-29 crewmen called *Accused American War Criminal* by Fiske Hanley?"

No, she had not read that book.

"What about *Knights of Bushido: A Short History of Japanese War Crimes* by Lord Edward F. Russell?"

She said she hadn't read that either.

"*Prisoners of the Japanese: POWs of World War II in the Pacific* by Gavan Daws? Have you read that?"

"No, Mr. Howell."

"Has anybody in Japan read anything about this? Is what your people did to American pilots and airmen like Bishop Watson vague to all of you?"

Mrs. Tashimoto did not respond.

"Are you familiar with other war crimes committed by your leaders and soldiers in World War II? How about the story told in the book *The Rape of Nanking* by Iris Chang? More than three hundred thousand Chinese civilians were systematically murdered. Thousands of women were raped. Civilians of all ages were beaten, water-tortured, used for karate practice, had their fingernails pulled out, forced to swallow lighted cigarettes—"

Radcliff objected, and Judge Lawton sustained the objection. Henry junior finally sat down.

But Radcliff, it turned out, had a counterattack. On redirect, he asked Mrs. Tashimoto to describe what it was like to be in Tokyo when the American bombers came at night and dropped their firebombs. At his prompting, she told of one horrible night in particular.

"A bomb from an American plane fell in the night on the house next to ours. It spewed out fire in all directions. I was down the street at my aunt's house where I was studying mathematics, and we all came running to see what had happened. The house and my family were already burning to the ground and the heavens by the time we arrived. So were other houses close by. The heat felt as if we had been put into an oven for baking bread or cakes. The sight and experience I will always remember is seeing my sister—she was fourteen years old—running out of the house and toward us. She was on fire. Her hair, her face, her body were ablaze. I will always remember the sight of that and the smell of burning human flesh—that of my own sister. I wanted to grab her and put the fire out, but she was so on fire I could not. I could only watch her burn to death.

"The fire, also, was sucking up the very air around us, and I was told to lie on the ground or I would suffocate to death. There was no real air to breathe, only fire air. Everyone in the house came out just as my sister did. All except my mother. The rest of us ran toward the river—the Sumida River—which was several blocks away. They said it was away from the fire and we could breathe. The streets were crowded with hundreds of people, all of them running for air and water and life as we were. We got to the river, but the bridge was too full of people, screaming and fighting and clawing. Many died right there in front of us and became bodies we had to run over or around. There were little children dead and old people dead. We kept running down the riverbank away from the bridge, and finally we got away from the smoke and the death.

"We went back to our neighborhood five days later, and all we found of my mother, once the fire was out and cold, were some of her burned bones. The next day my uncle took us to Kyoto, where we were told the Americans had decided not to bomb because of the temples and other religious shrines."

Then in an absolutely silent courtroom, Henry junior tried, on recross, a few last quiet shots.

"Mrs. Tashimoto, after there was the surrender and the peace, were you or any of your family bayoneted by the occupying American soldiers as your soldiers did the people of Nanking?"

No.

"Were you beaten or raped?"

No.

"Water-tortured?"

No.

"Used for karate or jujitsu practice?"

No.

"Were your fingernails pulled out?"

No.

"Were you forced to swallow lighted cigarettes?"

No.

"Is it correct to say that you were treated in a civilized manner at all times by all Americans?"

Yes.

"Based on your vague knowledge of the war, how did your treatment compare with that of women in countries such as China that were occupied by Japanese troops?"

"I don't know, Mr. Howell."

.   .   .

Mrs. Tashimoto moved Watson on.

Her bombing story caused him to spend the evening with an elderly Japanese man whose hair had been seared off so deeply from the skin on his body that Watson figured it would never grow back.

Elderly. Well, maybe not. Watson had always assumed he was an old man because he was thin and he seemed, like him, barely able to stand up without the help of a cane. His skin was scaled and hairless, so there was no other way to tell. But he might have been eighty or half that, or any age in between.

Watson was riding in a U.S. Army truck when he first saw the man. It was an afternoon in September 1945, a few days after Watson had been liberated from Camp Sengei 4. He and the other prisoners were examined by doctors aboard U.S. Navy ships and then brought back to port and put on trucks for a convoy ride to Atsugi Air Base near Tokyo. It was a large facility that had been converted quickly from a place where Japanese planes went off to kill Americans to one where American planes brought in occupying troops and supplies and left with POWs and other Americans who needed to go home.

Watson, weak and barely mobile, was given the best seat in the big four-by-four truck, up front on the passenger side. The driver was a brand-new army private, a healthy, husky kid from Utah who seemed uncomfortable, silenced by the presence of Watson and the damaged men from the prison camps.

The sights of a devastated Tokyo from the front seat of that truck were beyond anything Watson had imagined from his seat in *Big Red* thousands of feet above.

They drove down a main road that obviously had been recently cleared of rubble, which was heaped waist-high on both sides. It was mostly ashes, bricks, pieces of concrete and corrugated tin, burnt hunks of wood, rubber, and plaster. There were also the stark, twisted skeletons of vehicles—cars, trucks, buses, fire engines.

Watson assumed that deeper down in the rubble were the ashes and bones, shoes and clothes of incinerated human beings—Jap human beings.

Beyond the heaps lining the road there was nothing much to see except a few concrete chimneys and steel girders. Otherwise, it was all as level as a football field, as if no living or civilized things had ever been present. There were no trees or bushes, no buildings, no houses, no standing structures. Because of the debris it was hard to tell where there had once been streets going off this main road.

Bulldozers, their olive green paint already covered with grime and dust, were moving things around. Various odors combined to create an overpowering stench. The only thing even remotely similar Watson could recall was what he had sucked into his nostrils one afternoon when a grocery store two blocks away from his junior high school burned to the ground. Watson, only fourteen, went to the scene with some friends after the firemen got the blaze under control. He was jolted by the distinctive and blended odors of fried meat, eggs, fruit and vegetables; burnt milk, cocoa, and coffee;

melted soap and polishes; toasted bread, rolls, and cereals; singed wood and linoleum; shorted-out electrical and telephone wires. Nobody had died in the fire, so there had been no smell of human flesh. But this smell had human death in it. Many people had died in the firebombing that had reduced the city to waste, to chimneys, to dust, to nothing. John Quincy Watson, at the age of twenty-one, now was able to recognize the smell of dead humans.

Those people who had not died here in the fires that consumed their homes were gone now, as Watson and the trucks came through. There was no one around. If Watson hadn't known better, he could have thought nobody had ever lived here. How could they have? It was like a desert. What would they have used for shelter and nourishment? For life?

Watson had boarded that truck happy to be alive, happy to be a free man, on his way back home. He was happy to be an American, to be a man who had served his country as a pilot of a B-29 named *Big Red*.

Now he was also stunned, appalled, sickened by what he and his comrades and their B-29s had done to this city with their firebombs. He wished there had been another way for this truck convoy to get him to Atsugi and out of Japan without having to travel through this destroyed civilization.

Mostly, he wished that he had been left forever to his imaginings from five thousand feet, which had been bad enough, to remember what he had helped wreak on the people below. He had wondered then what it must have been like for them. Now he could no longer simply wonder.

Then up there in front of them appeared the scalded Japanese man standing on what used to be a street corner.

The kid from Utah said, "Look, Lieutenant, a live Jap!" He slowed the truck so they could get a better look at this live Jap, the only one they had seen since they left the port forty-five minutes before. Watson leaned out and forward through the open truck window.

The man—the man of indeterminate age—raised his right hand and shook his fist hard at Watson, at the truck, at the Americans, at everything. Watson got only a glimpse of the man's face and eyes, which seemed to shake and glow with anger. And then the truck passed on down the road and the man was out of Watson's sight.

But he was not gone.

That night on the flight in a C-54 transport plane from Atsugi to Iwo Jima—the first of four legs back to the States—Watson saw the man in a dream that was as real and horrible as anything he'd lived through since he and *Big Red* went down over Japan.

"I despise you, American flyer," said the man in perfect English. "I despise you, John Quincy Watson."

The man never came closer in the dream than the real man had been when the truck passed.

"How do you know my name?" Watson asked.

"It fell on us with your murderous fire."

"I am sorry."

"I am sorry I have no wife, no three daughters, no five grandchildren, no two brothers, no one sister, no seven nieces and nephews. I am sorry that you made me hate you, John Quincy Watson, for burning them up like the wood in our houses. I am sorry that I will never have peace as long as you live and they do not. I am sorry that I have no skin or hair on my body. I am sorry that I will hate you as long as you do have skin and hair on yours."

"You Japs did awful things to me."

"You will be punished, John Quincy Watson."

"The Hyena beat me and killed my comrades."

"What kind of animal name should I give you, John Quincy Watson?"

"I'm a fucky duck."

"You will be punished, Fucky Duck John Quincy Watson."

The dream came back—identical in both images and

words—on the second leg, from Iwo to Johnston Island, and on the third, to Oahu, Hawaii, and on the last, to Mather Air Base in California.

It came back repeatedly while he was in the San Antonio hospital, and it only began not to once he started his guilt sessions with Rick Allison. Finally, in the late sixties, some twenty years after that truck ride through Tokyo, it went away for good.

Now here it was again, as if the Japanese man with no skin or hair was right there in the room at the San Diego Sheraton alone with Watson.

"You will be punished, Fucky Duck John Quincy Watson," *the scalded man said.*

CHAPTER NINETEEN

Henry Howell, Jr., an inch taller than his father and his client, looked like a giant when he rose from the counsel table and declared in his boldest voice, "Your Honor, ladies and gentlemen of the jury, the defense calls as its first and only witness, the defendant, the Reverend John Quincy Watson, retired Methodist bishop of San Antonio, Texas."

The moment audiences everywhere had been waiting for had arrived. The bishop who had killed a man would now tell his story, explain himself, expose his mind and soul to the scrutiny of anyone who had access to a television or a radio. The white-walled courtroom, with its high ceilings and dark wood benches and trim, was no longer a place of justice. It was a stage, a studio, a backdrop of action and drama.

Watson was dressed in a solid dark blue suit, white shirt, wine-and-blue striped tie—typical of the way he dressed most Sunday mornings for the work he did in pulpits. He walked his usual slow pace to the witness stand, but it was definitely not for any false or staged effect. In fact, he wished he could have run up there so he could get it over with and behind him as quickly as possible.

There were some introductory questions about Watson's

leaving college to join the army, becoming a B-29 pilot, and being shot down after a bombing run over Tokyo. Henry junior, over the bishop's mild protest, had insisted that something be said about Watson's B-29 crew, a subject Watson would have preferred to skip over.

"How many of your crew survived the war, Bishop?"

"I was the only one."

Then began a recitation of the horrors.

Henry junior took the bishop through the details of the abuse and hurt he had witnessed and suffered personally at the hands of the Japanese, beginning with the whack to the head in the rice paddy and ending with the final brutalities at Sengei 4.

Watson spoke matter-of-factly, with little emphasis and no emotion, but the stories carried a punch simply in their telling.

"For most of us, sir," Henry junior said, "what you saw and endured is unimaginable."

"It had been unimaginable to me before it happened, Mr. Howell."

That exchange and the relentless recountings of beheadings, kicks, pummelings, and other tortures and indignities had a special poignance to many in the courtroom and the television audience. Almost everyone knew that along with John Quincy Watson, the father of the man asking the questions had endured the unimaginable.

"Bishop Watson, is this a photograph of you in 1943 when you received your wings as a pilot in the U.S. Army Air Forces?"

Yes, said Watson, barely glancing at the picture.

"How much did you weigh then?"

Around two hundred pounds.

"Is this a photograph taken of you shortly after you were liberated from that prison camp called Sengei 4?"

Yes, said Watson. His glance at this photo was even quicker.

"How much did you weigh then?"

One hundred and five pounds.

Henry junior then zeroed in on the Hyena, the other Tashimoto, the one who had inflicted so much of the pain and suffering on Watson and the others at Sengei 4.

That led to the specifics of the murder in San Diego. Bishop Watson, his firm voice faltering, said there had been no doubt in his mind that the man he saw first at the DFW airport and then in the Hotel Bayfront suite was the Hyena.

Why were you so sure?

"The eyes. I've never been able to put the sight and glare of those eyes out of my mind. They were his. I was certain they were his. Then when the gate agent at DFW confirmed that his name was Tashimoto, my certainty became a near absolute."

Henry junior asked the bishop to speak up if he could— some of his words were not being heard.

"This is very difficult for me, Mr. Howell," said the bishop.

"I know that, sir, I know that." And he asked Watson why he had followed the Japanese man to San Diego. "What was your purpose?"

"I had no specific purpose. I wanted to be with him, talk to him."

"Did you want to kill the Hyena?"

Watson raised his head and his voice: "No, no. Certainly not."

"You did not follow him with the express purpose of murdering him?"

"In the name of God, no, I did not." He spoke crisply and loudly.

"In the fifty years since you were set free from Japanese

captivity, did you ever try to find the Hyena—Lieutenant Tashimoto?"

"No," said Bishop Watson.

"Why not?" Henry junior asked.

"Because I thought he was dead."

"Why did you think that?"

Watson looked down at his right hand and the cane it was grasping. Then he raised his head and looked to his left straight at the jury and said, "Because I was one of those who had killed him."

Henry junior followed the bishop's lead and looked silently at the jury. There was the need for a dramatic pause—a slight break, a breath.

Then, the son of a man who was also there took the bishop through the story of the kicking death of the Hyena in the corpse shed.

"Have you ever told this story publicly or to any military or investigative body before today?" For the first time since the trial began, Henry junior's voice took on an intimate, personal tone. It was almost as if he and the bishop were suddenly speaking only to each other.

"No, I have not," Watson said.

"Why not, sir?"

"After the emotions of the act had passed, I felt tremendous shame and guilt for what I had done. I had committed murder. I also was overcome by enormous guilt for having enjoyed and felt good about committing such an act. In the rush of those moments in the shed, I had no doubt that the Hyena deserved to die for what he had done. It gave me great pleasure to be part of his execution. I hate to say it, but that is a fact."

With a series of friendly but pointed questions Henry junior, now back to his trial-lawyer manner, pressed hard on why Watson brushed aside Bill Joe Tashimoto's repeated denials that he was the Hyena.

"I didn't believe him," Watson explained, "because, as I said, the eyes and everything else seemed to match. I thought he was in a permanent state of denial. I asked him to come to terms with who he was and what he had done, but he declined on grounds that he had done nothing wrong to me or anyone else."

"He said he was in Singapore during the war?"

"Yes. He said he worked as an interpreter."

"But whatever he said, you remained convinced he was the Hyena, the man who had been at Sengei 4?"

"Firmly and absolutely so."

Then came the hard part.

"Why did you kill Bill Joe Tashimoto, Bishop?"

Watson retrieved a white handkerchief from his suit-coat pocket and ran it slowly over his mouth and nose before answering, "He kicked me, karate-style, in my groin—my private parts. It hurt and angered me so that I flew into an uncontrollable rage."

Henry junior paused for two beats so the jury and all others listening could imagine the pain. Then he asked, "Do you remember thinking, I will now kill this man who has repeated his most grievous offense against my body?"

"I had no thoughts. I only acted."

Another pause while Henry junior looked at the jury and nodded in a show of understanding. *It makes sense to me, doesn't it also to you, ladies and gentlemen of the jury?* That was his message.

"You broke his neck with your own two hands," Henry junior said. "Where did you learn how to do that? Were you trained in the U.S. Army to do such things?"

The bishop's voice faltered again as he answered. "No. That was not part of a B-29 pilot's training. My only exposure to that awful act was when I witnessed the Hyena employ it on a British prisoner at Sengei 4."

Henry junior boomed back: "It had left such an impression that it remained there for reflexive, automatic use after more than fifty years?"

"That appears to be the only explanation," the bishop quietly replied.

"Why did you throw him off the balcony?"

"Again, I don't recall making a concrete decision about it. I just did it. The rage must have still been in charge of my emotions and actions."

Henry junior nodded again to the jury. Then he looked back at the bishop and took matters to a rapid, uninterrupted conclusion.

"Do you regret having taken the life of Bill Joe Tashimoto?"

"With every ounce of energy that is in me. I have expressed this publicly to Mrs. Tashimoto and to her family. It was a terrible thing that I did. It runs counter to everything I believe and stand for as a human being and a Christian."

"Would you feel the same remorse if it had, in fact, been the *real* Lieutenant Tashimoto, the *real* Hyena?"

"I hope I would, but I honestly do not know. There are forces still in me, it turns out, that I had thought were long gone. I do not have the control over myself that I believed—and took for granted—my Christian faith and good common sense had given me. I had not realized how deeply the seeds of hate and violence were planted in me by that experience fifty years ago."

It was there that Henry junior ended his direct examination of the bishop.

Judge Lawton pounded the gavel for a noon recess, and the reporters left the courtroom with a new lead: Watson admits to kicking Japanese officer to death!

.   .   .

The afternoon cross-examination began slowly with prosecutor Radcliff attempting to knock down the bishop's point that he really couldn't help himself that evening at the Hotel Bayfront.

"Yesterday morning," Radcliff began, "in a well-publicized sermon at a church here in San Diego, you said, 'Let no man or woman ever say, 'The Devil made me do it.' Isn't that exactly what you just did?"

Bishop Watson reminded the district attorney that he also said in that sermon that he was mortal and not able to always practice what he preached.

Radcliff took a quick hit on something else: "By your own admission, you killed a man fifty years ago and got a huge kick out of it—no pun intended. Did you enjoy your second murder as much?"

"I don't remember having any such feeling," the bishop answered.

Radcliff extended his arms, placed his hands on the table in front of him, and leaned forward toward the bishop as far as he could. "Tell us again why you killed Bill Joe Tashimoto."

Watson blanched as if hit by a strong wind. Clearly he didn't want to say it all again. But he had to. "As I said, he kicked me in the groin, which sent my memory and my soul into an uncontrollable rage." He said it matter-of-factly, almost as if by rote.

"Did you not stalk him from the Dallas–Fort Worth airport to his hotel room in San Diego like a hunter going after a three-point buck for the kill?"

"I said I did not, and I did not." His head was down slightly now, and so was his voice.

"A hypothetical question, Bishop. Let's say you went to that room to visit with an old friend or a even a fellow minister or retired bishop. Let's say something came up between you that turned to violence. Let's say it got so violent that the other man kicked you in your groin. Would you have broken his neck and then, to make sure, tossed him off an eighteenth-floor balcony?"

Strongly, with indignation, the bishop replied, "No! I'm sure I wouldn't have reacted that way."

"What if you were attacked in the same way by a total stranger? Would you have broken his neck and thrown him onto the concrete patio of the Hotel Bayfront?"

"No!" The word shot through the courtroom. But once it was said, the bishop's shoulders and face sagged as if they were balloons leaking air.

It was well into the afternoon by now, almost four o'clock. Henry junior stood and asked if there might be a recess until the morning. The judge asked Radcliff what he thought of the idea.

"Just one more series of questions, Your Honor, and I believe we can finish our cross-examination this afternoon," Radcliff replied.

"Fine," said the judge. But she proclaimed a fifteen-minute recess before continuing.

.   .   .

His crew.

Fifty years later, Watson knew very little about what had happened to the ten other men who were with him in *Big Red* that night over Tokyo.

None of them ever showed up at Sengei 4, and that was the only thing Watson knew for sure until the war was over. While still in Japan he inquired about them, and after liberation he looked around for their faces on navy ships and again on the transport planes and everywhere he passed through on his way home. He saw none of them, and neither had anyone else he asked.

At Brooke he demanded immediately that somebody please find out for him what had happened to his ten comrades. Fortunately, his plea eventually ended up with Dave Cantrell, a master sergeant in the administration office at nearby Fort Sam Houston. Cantrell, a career army man, brought an answer soon, several days before the war-crimes trio came to call on Watson.

"All are listed officially as missing, sir," said the sergeant, a pleasant, competent man from North Carolina who said he had spent most of the war with the 36th Infantry Division in France.

"Did you check the lists of released prisoners of war?" Watson asked.

"I did, sir."

"What about those who died as prisoners?"

"It'll be a while before we get anything like that, sir. It's possible we may never know about all of them."

"People can't just disappear without a trace, can they?"

"Well, Lieutenant, I would guess you can answer that question about these particular men a lot better than I can," said the sergeant.

Yes, sergeant, you are absolutely correct, Watson thought. They could have died instantly right there on the plane. Or been tossed from the plane unconscious and thus unable to use their parachutes. Or gotten tangled up in the plane on the way out. Or parachuted down safely but landed in water, never to be rescued. Or landed on ground and been killed by Japanese civilians or soldiers or snakes or whatever. They could have been unable to get out of the plane and gone down with it, alive, in flames, wherever it crashed. Into a hillside, a rice paddy, or the Sea of Japan.

Yes, sergeant, these ten people could have just disappeared without a trace.

But *I* made it. Why didn't any of the others? I was their commander. Maybe it was because I was the last one out of the plane. Maybe I was lucky that I came down where I did . . .

Lucky.

Three months after he arrived at Brooke, Watson got
Master Sergeant Cantrell to give him a list of the names and
addresses of the ten men's next of kin. Then, with the help of
Rick Allison and Joyce, he wrote ten letters. In each he
praised the son—in two cases it was a husband—for his
skills as a crewman on a B-29 and for his bravery and valor
under fire. He told about the collision with a Jap fighter—
whether it was an intentional ramming or accident of combat and darkness, he did not know—and the danger, chaos,
and tragedy that followed.

He said nothing in any of the letters about the fact that no
one else in the crew of *Big Red* but him appeared to have
survived the war. It was simply too difficult to put in writing
for anyone—particularly the family of one who had not
come out alive—to read.

Watson's last sentence was the same in each: "I join you in
hoping and praying that sometime before too long we will be
able to obtain some authoritative information as to exactly
what happened to your son (husband)."

Once the letters were written and mailed, the fate of his
crew then became another of the awful haunts Watson
worked at putting behind him and out of his mind and soul.

It wasn't until the spring of 1948, while in Dallas at seminary, that it returned the first time. He received a brief handwritten note from Master Sergeant Cantrell, who was now
on duty at the Pentagon in Washington. "Two of your men
turned up on this terrible list," wrote the sergeant. "Their
families have been officially notified." The note was clipped
to a sheath of official-looking papers. They were an account
from the War Crimes Trial Record of five Japanese accused
of massacring American prisoners of war.

One of the prosecutors wrote in the report:

The study of wartime atrocities perpetrated by the Japanese has brought to light numerous fiendish and barbaric

acts, but few of these can attain the diabolical depths reached by the acts surrounding the tragedy that took place in May 1945 at the Tokyo Military Prison. On that fateful night of 25–26 May 1945, there were confined in this prison at Shibuya, Tokyo, 62 American flyers, ranging in rank or grade from private first class to lieutenant colonel, all of whom had been shot down while engaged in bombing operations over Japan. Of this number, 45 have been positively identified—at the same time there were also confined at that prison some 450 to 500 Japanese military and political prisoners.

On the morning of 26 May at 0300 hours there was not an American alive of these 62. All had perished by fire or sword during a fire brought about by an incendiary air raid that burned the prison to the ground. Of all the Japanese prisoners incarcerated in the prison at the time, not a single one of them perished, since all had been safely evacuated to places outside the prison area during the night.

The 62 Americans were not allowed to seek refuge from the fire and 17 of those who attempted to flee the fire and certain death were struck down and murdered by prison guards.

The last page of the report was a list of the forty-five victims thus far identified. The master sergeant had underlined two of the names: "2nd Lt. Mark Luther Parish—Martinsburg, W. Va." and "S.Sgt. Richard Leon Malone—Salem, Oregon." Parish had been Watson's bombardier; Malone was the radar operator.

So, at least two of the ten had also successfully bailed out. So the Hyena was right when he told Watson that first day he was lucky and fortunate to have been a prisoner of his at Sengei 4? It was, for Watson, a question with no answer.

Those kinds of thoughts lingered with him only a day or

two because by then he was well into his theology studies, his life and hopes as a would-be minister of the Lord and as the husband of Joyce. He couldn't even immediately remember exactly what Parish and Malone looked like and decided not to push his memory.

The crew haunt returned only one more time. That happened on a Sunday morning in June 1985, after he delivered a guest sermon at the First Methodist Church of Kansas City, Missouri. A tiny, frail woman, about his age, came up to him at a small reception the church held afterward for Watson, the visiting bishop of San Antonio.

"My husband was Tom Southard," said the woman, who couldn't have been much taller than five feet or weighed more than ninety pounds.

Watson couldn't place the name.

"You wrote me a letter about him," said the woman.

A letter? I wrote a letter about a Tom Southard? Watson ran his memory back through his various ministerial assignments. Could it have been in Del Rio? Seguin? In Austin, maybe?

Watson was struck by the look of deep disappointment on the woman's face at his inability to recall her husband. "I'm so sorry," he said. "In my work as a minister, I come in contact with so many people."

"Tom was your copilot, Bishop," she said. Her voice was flat and soft but forceful. She was clearly someone who was used to being listened to.

He took her hands in his and then wrapped his arms around her, enveloping her in an embrace that made her all but disappear inside him. "Oh, my Lord, yes. Southie. We called him Southie. He was a wonderful man, a truly wonderful man."

He quickly excused himself from the others at the reception and took the woman to a quiet corner in the church social hall, where they sat down together on a leather couch.

She said her name was Janet—Janet Anderson now. She had married a second time, to a man named Roger Anderson, who had died of a stroke two years ago. She said she lived in Warrensburg, a town west of Kansas City where she had been born and raised and had gone back to live when Tom went overseas. They had met at the University of Missouri at Columbia while studying to be math teachers. They had married four weeks before he left for Saipan.

"I'm still in Warrensburg teaching algebra and geometry to kids who wish they were somewhere else," she told Watson. "Tom and I had planned to move to a city and teach together—here to Kansas City or maybe even someplace like Chicago. But after he didn't come home I just decided to stay put."

She said she was a Methodist and had seen in her district newsletter that Bishop Quincy Watson was preaching here this morning. The biography said Watson had been a B-29 pilot in World War II, so she had decided to drive over and introduce herself—and see if he was the same person Tom had flown with.

"The second I saw you, I knew you were the right one," she said. "Tom said you were tall."

Watson remembered Southie better than the others because their jobs up there in the cockpit—the greenhouse—were so connected and related and that made them very dependent on each other. Southie had been small—five feet eight or so, and thin—or so he recalled. But almost everyone seemed small to John Quincy Watson.

"We flew well together, your husband and I—almost as one," Watson said. "We got so we could communicate with our eyes up there when there was no time or it was too noisy to talk."

He told her about how the two of them approached every bombing-mission takeoff from Saipan as if it were the most important event in their lives. Their plane was always overloaded with bombs and fuel, and the margin of error was dangerously small rolling down the runway for liftoff.

"Southie talked us through it. I can hear him now. 'Airspeed. Forty . . . fifty . . . sixty . . . eighty . . . You're too far to the right, Quincy . . . ninety . . . correction okay . . . steady . . . one-thirty . . . one-forty . . . liftoff . . . fifty feet . . . gear coming up . . . level out . . . one-sixty . . .' His voice was so soft and calm, so easy to listen to, so normal—it became so necessary to me."

He explained that he and Southie functioned as pilot and copilot even though the army, because of the complications of the B-29, invented the job of aircraft commander, or AC, to replace the official pilot's title. She knew her husband's official title was that of pilot even though his job was that of a copilot.

"So he sat on the right and you on the left?" she asked.

Watson said that was correct.

"I always imagined him being someday on the left—in the driver's seat."

"We literally shared the driver's seat, Mrs. Anderson."

Then she asked Watson if he minded telling her what he remembered about those final moments aboard *Big Red*. She said she had gone on with her life after the war but had never forgotten Tom. She still wanted to know everything there was to know about him and his death.

Watson had been so successful in putting his haunts and nightmares behind him, he had trouble at first honoring her request. He had been surprised at how he was able to suddenly describe the takeoff, but this was different. He stumbled over some of the details of the collision with the Jap fighter, the smoke in the cockpit, and the decision to bail out.

"Was Tom alive when you last saw him?" she asked.

Watson was tempted to lie. To say that Southie was killed

instantly—and mercifully—in the initial collision. But he couldn't do that to this woman. Only the truth would do for Janet Anderson.

"Yes," he said. "He gave me a thumbs-up and headed back to the bomb-bay door to parachute out."

"He wasn't hurt?"

"No, not that I could tell."

"Did you actually see him jump out of the plane?"

"No. I was still in the cockpit."

"Why didn't the two of you go together?"

"My job was to be the last out."

Janet Anderson spoke quietly but with determination. He had the feeling that she had been working on these questions and waiting to ask them of somebody for a long time. She had not put her haunts behind *her*.

She said, "I wrote many letters to the War Department— then the Defense Department and the army—and later the Air Force—trying to get information about what might have happened to Tom. They never came up with anything other than he was still missing. What do you think happened to him, Bishop?"

Well, there it was. There was *the* question she drove over from Warrensburg this Sunday morning to ask.

Watson went through the possibilities as gently as he could. Instant death had been eliminated. So, the first was that Southie, like him, had been captured by the Japanese but did not survive captivity.

"Why wouldn't there be a record of that somewhere, then?" she asked. "They told me over and over that Tom's name was not on any of the Japanese lists but that there were some prisoners they had that were never accounted for."

Watson said he had heard that as well. He mentioned Parish and Malone, whose names turned up later on the Tokyo Military Prison massacre list. He said it was possible even that Tom was was also a victim of that atrocity—but had never been identified.

"Why weren't the Japanese made to account for all of our prisoners after the war?" she asked. "Why didn't we make them own up to what they had done?"

Watson said he had often wondered the same thing.

"When I hear all of these shrieking women on television talking about their MIAs in Vietnam I want to yell at them, 'My Tom has been missing for forty years and nobody ever cared or looked for him.' But there's no need to harbor that kind of feeling. As a preacher, you certainly know that."

Janet Anderson's eyes—they were a stunning blue—flashed with an anger that, it seemed clear to Watson, would never go away.

He acknowledged that he had had his own troubles dealing with the fact that nobody seemed to much care what had happened to him in a Japanese prison camp.

She asked him if his use of a cane was the result of anything the Japanese had done. He told her some of the story of Sengei 4—the whacking of his leg and right ear—but made no mention of the kicking.

She responded, "People like us embarrass other people, Bishop. I read that somewhere, and I believe it. When a war is over everybody wants the wounded and the widows and the other hurt people to go away and stay out of sight so everybody can forget how horrible it all was."

Watson said that was probably right.

"Did they give you any medals, Bishop Watson?" she asked.

Watson told her about the Purple Heart and the Air Medal.

"They sent me Tom's Purple Heart in the mail," she said. "I put it on the mantel in my parents' home and kept it there with Tom's picture for a while. Then when I married Roger I put it in a drawer. Some antiques dealer offered me fifty dollars for it. Can you imagine people buying and selling dead men's medals—Purple Hearts particularly?"

Watson said he couldn't.

Janet Anderson opened her small gray leather purse and pulled out what appeared to be a V-mail letter, the thin blue stationery made especially for personal mail during World War II. The paper was blank on one side for writing and then could be folded up with lines for the address showing on the outside. She unfolded it and handed it to Watson. "You're mentioned there in the third paragraph."

Watson took the letter, found the paragraph, and read, "The luckiest thing we have going for us is Quincy Watson, our real Big Red. He's a big man in so many ways—tall as a tree, smart as Einstein, grand as a sunset. He's no older than me but he seems like he's as wise as God. He's also such a natural pilot you'd think he was born up in the sky somewhere. I can't imagine anything bad happening to us as long as he's in charge of our airplane."

Watson handed the letter back to Janet Anderson and burst into tears.

.   .   .

There were actual groans heard in the courtroom after the judge called court back into session and Radcliff said, "Now, continuing our cross-examination, Bishop Watson. You committed one murder fifty years ago and another three months ago. Have there been any others?"

"Certainly not!" The two words boomed out of the bishop's mouth.

Radcliff smiled slightly. "I would ask, sir, that you think again about that. Let me ask you the question again: Have you committed any other murders?"

Henry junior was now on his feet in full thunder.

"Your Honor, please, this is an outrage! To suggest in front of the jury that Bishop Watson is some kind of serial killer is absurd and reprehensible!"

The judge told Henry junior to calm down and told the bishop to answer the question.

Watson, still at full boom, said, "If you are referring to the Japanese who may have died as the result of the bombs we dropped from our B-29, then yes. I have committed other murders. I deeply regret the death and destruction that those bombs caused to so many innocent civilians. But I do not consider that murder. It was done in the course of my duties as an officer in the U.S. Army in war against a declared enemy of my country. That does not excuse, but I believe it certainly explains."

"No, Bishop, that was not what I had in mind. I don't believe any American would ever consider what you did to end the war as murder. I was thinking of an Australian commando lieutenant at Sengei 4 named Matt McCory. Do you remember him?"

There was absolute silence. The look on the bishop's face was that of someone who had just been slapped.

"Did you not hear my question, Bishop Watson?"

In a barely audible whisper, the bishop said, "I heard your question."

"What is your answer, sir?"

"No."

"No? Did you say no?"

"We mostly went by nicknames, and it's been fifty years."

"Do you remember being called out of a prison formation one morning to assist the Hyena in the killing of an Australian officer?"

There was silence again. The bishop lowered his head. It was hard to see if his eyes were open or shut.

"Your head is down, Bishop. I can't see your face. Are you talking? Are you answering?"

The bishop's lips were not moving. His whole body was perfectly still.

"I have here in my hand a deposition of man named Lee D. Peacock. It was taken by officials of the U.S. embassy in Canberra, Australia, three days ago. It says he saw this trial on Australian television and it brought back to him the memory of an incident that he witnessed while a prisoner at Sengei 4 in the summer of 1945. I can go through the process of having it entered in evidence, or you can tell us what happened. It's your call, Bishop."

"I will tell you what happened."

And Watson did.

When he was finished, Henry junior asked no redirect questions. In a much quieter voice than he'd begun with, he announced that the defense rested.

.   .   .

The Australian was a lieutenant, a man in his late twenties who had been badly wounded in the head and stomach and captured during some kind of commando raid that went awry off the coast of Japan. He could barely move or speak and was clearly headed for death from the day he arrived at Sengei 4. The rest of the prisoners saw it as a miracle each morning this brave, stubborn Aussie remained alive.

Henry praised Matt McCory's courage and determination and cited him repeatedly to them all as the ultimate example of a man refusing to die.

On July 7, 1945—Watson could never forget the date—the Hyena called McCory's name at morning formation. He was the one chosen to die this morning, and even his will wasn't strong enough to keep it from happening.

It took three Jap soldiers to help the Aussie to the killing spot in front of the two Japanese officers. They pushed him to his knees, but there was no wooden block there. The Hyena had chosen a new method this morning. He looped a long piece of rope around the commando's neck and then had two Japanese soldiers pull on the ends with all their might. They yanked like two tug-of-war competitors, the obvious object being to break McCory's neck or strangle him to death. But the victim just refused to die. The Jap soldiers pulled and pulled, and McCory remained stubbornly upright and alive. Even when the Hyena, frustrated, pushed one of the soldiers aside and began yanking on the rope himself, Matt McCory, Australian commando, still would not fall.

Suddenly, the Hyena turned around to the rest of the prisoners.

"Lieutenant Watson, front and center!" he screamed.

"So long, Quincy," Henry said.

"Call my family in Connecticut," said Watson. "Thomas Alfred Watson in Westbrook. They're in the book."

"Will do."

So his day to die had finally come—that was the way Watson saw it as he limped out toward the terrible scene. His determination to survive, almost as strong as McCory's by now, likewise was not enough to forestall the Hyena's determination to kill them, one at a time.

He handed Watson the rope. Watson didn't take it; he bowed slightly and smiled as he called the Hyena a *mendula fellator cunnus* out loud. The Hyena angrily tried to jam the rope into Watson's right hand. Watson would not clasp his fingers around it, and it fell to the ground.

That brought the Hyena to a high state of cackle. He did a military pirouette and faced Watson's fellow special prisoners of Sengei 4. He laughed a little bit more and then in his highest pitch said to them, "I could, of course, put this poor man here on his knees out of his misery. He has but a short time to live in any case. I have the means of sword and pistol to end his life and to do so quickly. But I have elected not to do that. I have instead chosen Lieutenant Watson to assist in finishing this task in the fashion that I wish. But as you can see, he has declined to participate. Let me see if I can offer an incentive for him to do so. If he does cooperate with me on this project, no one else will die today or tomorrow. If he does not, another of you will be called forward immediately. So the future of one of you is in the hands of redheaded Lieutenant Watson. Does he trade the life of this dying man—I can assure you he will die today no matter the method—for the life of one of you?"

"Do it, Quincy!" Henry yelled from the ranks.

"Go ahead, mate!" yelled one of the other Australians. "He's a goner no matter what."

Several similar shouts rose in a variety of accents, tones, and pitches.

Watson picked up the rope and, with a Japanese soldier holding the other end, pulled it hard. He heard a slight cracking sound, and McCory fell forward, dead—finally.

The Hyena cackled louder and more exuberantly than Watson had ever heard him laugh.

Watson and the others then watched in unspeakable horror as the Hyena walked over to the front rank of the prisoners, pointed at one to step forward, called him Fucky Duck, and shot him in the head. The man, a B-29 bombardier named Rhodes, dropped straight down dead. Watson knew him; he had been on the burial detail. Watson remembered his talking about his plan to go to school on the G.I. Bill to become a pharmacist like his father, who had promised to add "& Son" to the name of the family drugstore back home in southern Illinois.

Not even in Latin were there adequate words to describe the hate Watson felt at that moment for the Hyena—and for himself.

Fifty years later, as he finished telling the world the story in a San Diego courtroom, the feeling returned and lingered.

CHAPTER TWENTY

The end came quickly.

At 9:00 A.M. sharp Judge Lawton banged the gavel to call the court to order and told District Attorney Radcliff to give his closing argument to the jury.

As he had done throughout the trial, Radcliff, like the football player he had been, came at everything head on.

"No, ladies and gentlemen of the jury, I do not stand here to pronounce John Quincy Watson a serial killer, a maniac who needs to be locked up before he kills again."

He took a long pause, ran his right hand—his pass-throwing hand—through his thinning, dark blond hair, and looked right at the bishop for several seconds before saying, "No, when I look at the defendant I see a distinguished American who, as a young man, served his country with gallantry and courage. He flew a B-29 Superfortress, the bombs dropped by him and his crew over Japan having helped bring the bloodshed of World War II to an end. He parachuted into enemy territory, was captured and then underwent unspeakable mistreatment and injury as a Japanese prisoner of war."

Then in the great on-the-other-hand tradition of criminal-case jury summations to taketh away what one has just giveth, Radcliff increased the tempo of his speech. "Yes, he did, by his own admission, participate in the stomping to death of a man he knew as the Hyena at the end of the war. I will leave that to the military and others to resolve, but from my vantage point, 'not guilty' is the verdict."

Looking at Watson, he continued, "What ever you did to that terrible man, Bishop, so be it. It is history and the case is closed. We admire your candor in telling us about it."

Radcliff, his tanned outdoorsy face turning to a worried frown, was not so charitable about the Australian commando. He conceded that Watson pulled the rope in the belief and hope that in doing so he might help spare the lives of some of his fellow prisoners. While again leaving the judgment about that to others, he took a whack at the bishop's initial lack of candor about it.

Then came the final spinning pitch—pass, in football terms: "No, ladies and gentlemen of the jury, the issue before you now is not three murders—it is only one. It's the cold-blooded murder of Bill Joe Tashimoto, an innocent man from Japan who just happened to be in the wrong airport at the wrong time. I say to you with every ounce of candor *I* can muster, that John Quincy Watson is, to use the mixed cliché of his line of work and mine, guilty as sin. He must be found guilty of murder in the second degree as charged and sent to prison."

Radcliff, now slowly pacing in front of the jury box, repeated his view that it would be absurd to consider either self-defense or "the Devil made me do it" as a way out for Bishop Watson.

Then, after stopping to stare at them for a silent count of four, he took a crack at Henry junior and the defense team.

"I'm sure you found it as distasteful as I did the way the defense suggested that maybe—just maybe—Bill Joe Tashimoto was involved in atrocities such as terrible medical ex-

periments on prisoners of war in Singapore. They offered no
evidence of that, of course, but that did not prevent them
from pretty much saying, 'Oh, well, the bishop got the
wrong Tashimoto, but so what? All Tashimotos deserve to
die anyhow. What's the problem?' That's racism, my fellow
Americans, pure and simple—*that's* the problem. And that's
the *best* thing I can say about it."

Radcliff, dressed in a perfectly cut three-button gray char-
coal suit, stuck his hands in his trouser pockets and looked
at the jurors—one face at a time. It took several silent seconds to cover all twelve. Then, slowly, he spoke the final
words of condemnation. "Ladies and gentlemen, whatever
John Quincy Watson had been before that fateful evening
here in San Diego, he was at that particular moment in time
a determined killer. At first he did not succeed, so he tried
again."

He removed his hands from his pockets, buttoned the
middle button on his coat, walked right up to the jury box,
and said, "There is no alternative to a verdict of guilty. Our
system of self-government is dependent on the citizens doing
their duty when it calls. Today, ladies and gentlemen, it calls
you. Thank you for your service to justice, San Diego
County, and the state of California."

Somebody in the audience broke into applause. Then another person joined in. The judge angrily banged the gavel
for silence and warned against any other such outbursts.

Henry junior waited several seconds after that before
standing and approaching the jury box to make his summa-
tion. He wanted there to be a punctuation of silence between
what he and Radcliff had to say. The pause helped also to es-
tablish a physical contrast between him and Radcliff. Henry
junior was more than four inches taller than Radcliff and, at
nearly 225 pounds, at least 35 pounds heavier. He had been
a wrestler in college, but if he had played football he would

have been a defensive lineman or linebacker, certainly not a strutting dandy of a quarterback.

With no words of introduction or salutation, he faced the jurors with his huge legs slightly apart and spoke with a force that almost rattled the water glasses on the counsel tables.

"The district attorney speaks of distaste for something my defense team has done. He accuses us of racism, of suggesting that Bill Joe Tashimoto deserved to die. That is an outrageous distortion of what transpired in this courtroom. It is a damnable lie, ladies and gentlemen. I know you know it because you heard everything that was said. I merely wanted to express my disappointment with the smears of the prosecutor, this representative of the people."

He eyeballed each of the twelve jurors while they paused to reflect on what he had just said before he continued. "The district attorney of your county, in his zeal to get a conviction, has engaged in some despicable rhetoric, the kind that feeds the public's distrust of lawyers. He says: 'I do not stand here to pronounce John Quincy Watson a serial killer, a maniac who needs to be locked up before he kills again.' *Please!* That is exactly what he is telling you and what he wants you to believe.

"Tipped off by someone in Australia, he springs this so-called third murder on the bishop and then tries to act as if it does not matter, as if it should not be considered in your deliberations. If it didn't matter, then why in the name of fairness and justice did he bring it up? Oh, it matters all right. Because he wants you to believe Bishop Watson is some kind of racist fiend, a man who if set free will walk through the airports of America looking for people to murder—most particularly people who are or look Japanese."

He moved back to the counsel table, faced the seated Bishop Watson for a few seconds, and then turned toward the jurors again. Pointing to Watson, he said, "I would ask that you attempt the impossible: Try to put yourself in the place of this man, Bishop John Quincy Watson." He lowered his hand and returned to a spot less than a yard from the jury box. "For fifty years you have suffered from the crimes against your body and soul that were committed by an animal of a man named Tashimoto. For fifty years you thought that terrible person, the man you called the Hyena, had been punished for his crimes. You thought he was dead. Then one day out of the blue at the Dallas–Fort Worth airport, you see him. There he is! The animal who made it impossible for you to have children! The animal who made it mandatory that you walk with a cane!"

Henry junior raised his right leg and kicked it into the air. "That animal strikes out again, landing a solid blow in your groin, the very place where so much lasting damage and hurt was inflicted fifty years ago."

He leaned forward and shouted, "You are suddenly in a rage of fire, a rage of hate, a rage that has been dormant for fifty years! You strike out! You kill!"

Henry walked to one end of the jury box and back to the other end and then returned to his position in the center. In a subdued voice he said, "You immediately turn yourself in to the police and tell the complete story of what happened in that hotel suite and why. You are overcome with remorse and guilt for having mistakenly ended the life of a man named Bill Joe Tashimoto."

Hands extended in front him palms up, he asked, "Do you deserve to be labeled a murderer? Do you deserve to go to prison?

"I say no. The prosecutor has taken it upon himself to pronounce verdicts. I will do the same. I say you are not guilty under the laws of California and of mankind. And if *you* are so, then Bishop John Quincy Watson must also be so."

Henry junior thanked the twelve citizens of San Diego

County for their service, bowed his head slightly in respect for them, and returned slowly, heavily to the defense table and sat down.

Again, there was applause from some spectators. "Bravo!" a man shouted. "Amen!" a woman yelled.

The judge, her pale white face reddening, banged her gavel. She ordered the bailiff and the several uniformed deputy sheriffs in the courtroom to remove anyone who made another sound. The courtroom went stone silent.

And then a sudden realization that this trial was almost over seemed to cause everyone in the room to take a collective breath—and to hold it.

The judge, a small, black-haired woman in her late fifties who never smiled, gave her instructions to the jury. Most of it dealt with defining the difference, under the law, between murder in the second degree and voluntary manslaughter. She told them not to consider the differences each finding would mandate in sentences. If a guilty verdict was returned, there would be a separate phase for them to consider the sentence.

It was, according to the clock on the wall behind the judge's bench, 11:26 A.M. when the jury of seven men and five women retired to consider their verdict.

Forty-five minutes later a bailiff informed the judge that the jury had reached that verdict.

Less than thirty minutes after that, the courtroom refilled with all the players, including the bishop and the lawyers as well as the reporters, bailiffs, and the regulars from the public that a trial of this kind always attracts.

"Ladies and gentlemen of the jury, I have been told that you have reached a verdict," said the judge. "Is that correct?"

"It is, Your Honor," said the foreman, a middle-aged white man in an orange sport shirt.

The judge asked the bailiff to take and pass her the paper with the verdict. She unfolded it and said,

"Bishop Watson, will you please stand."

Even on television, the enormity of the moment to this man was evident. To those in the courtroom, there seemed a new layer of age to his face, a new expectation that another difficulty was coming into his life, and a new resignation to the fact that he was powerless to stop it.

The judge read, "In the case of the *People of California versus John Quincy Watson,* we the jury find the defendant not guilty of second-degree murder. We instead find the defendant guilty of voluntary manslaughter."

The courtroom was full of confusion. Was this a good verdict, a bad verdict? Who won, who lost? Nobody seemed to know whether to clap or hiss.

Bishop Watson, still standing, lowered his head, closed his eyes, and shook his head back and forth twice.

Then Henry Howell, Sr., his friend and fellow former POW, came up and put his arm around Watson's shoulder.

"All the way to the U.S. Supreme Court is where we go now, Bishop Fucky Duck," Howell said to Watson. "They are not going to get away with this."

Almost immediately Henry junior said to the judge, "If Your Honor please, we ask that the defendant remain free on bail while various motions are prepared and filed."

The judge asked prosecutor Radcliff if he had any objection.

"I think, Your Honor, that Bishop Watson is a special case and not a likely candidate for fleeing the country or the jurisdiction of this court," said Radcliff, smiling broadly and making no effort to hide his happiness with the verdict.

But then Henry junior, who had been in a furious conversation with his client and his father, said to the judge, "At the insistence of my client and against my advice and protest, Your Honor, I hereby withdraw my request for the continuation of the bond—and Bishop Watson's freedom."

That set the courtroom off into a buzz of whispers, sighs, coughs. What did this mean? Nobody seemed to know.

Watson was immediately handcuffed and taken by three San Diego County sheriff's deputies to the county jail. Henry senior went with him and, upon arrival, asked that he be allowed a few minutes of privacy with Bishop Watson.

The request was granted—again by special exception—and they were locked inside a small room used by lawyers to talk to their jailed clients. They sat across from each other at a gray metal table. For the next ninety minutes, they talked. Sometimes the words came in screams that brought jailers on the run to unlock the door to make sure no harm was being committed.

The issue between the two friends was filing an immediate motion for a new trial, giving notice of appeal, and then appealing the verdict forever to each and every appropriate court in the land, including the U.S. Supreme Court, if necessary.

"No," said Quincy. "There will be none of that."

"Yes," said Henry. "There will be *all* of that."

Watson tried to look away. There was no way to turn his head far enough in any direction to escape the other big man's gaze. He said, "It's my decision, not yours."

Henry, his aging hulk of a body leaning even closer over at Quincy's aging hulk, said, "It's my friend, not yours."

Watson was tired, done. "Henry, please. I murdered a man. A jury says I must be punished. That is the judgment against me, and I must accept it. So be it."

Henry was not close to done. "Juries are often wrong—look at O.J. and ten thousand other cases I could cite with a little help from a law student. So be *that*."

"I deserve to be punished. I should have simply pled guilty at the beginning—"

"Oh, please, save me that crap. Punished? What in the hell do you think that was you went through—*we* went through—at the hands of the Hyena? You have been punished more than enough for a hundred murders, Quincy. Get off that preacher shit, please. We're talking here about your life."

Watson was not about to argue "preacher shit" with Henry. They had already done that many times, particularly during the Vietnam War. Henry had been a pro-LBJ hawk, Watson an antiwar supporter of Eugene McCarthy, a real oddity in Texas at the time. But his congregation in San Antonio, one of Texas's most tolerant and liberal cities despite its many military installations, didn't mind, and neither did anybody else. But Henry Howell, otherwise a liberal Democrat, minded. He could not understand how a man who had been a B-29 commander and suffered as a prisoner in a war against fascism could not rally to Johnson's call to do the same against communism. Watson said it was a matter of conscience and common sense. Who knows better than the two of us the horrors of war, Henry? he had asked. Who knows better than the two of us the dangers of killer fanatics? Henry replied.

"My life is over anyhow, Henry," Watson said now in the little room at the San Diego County Jail.

"If you go to prison, you're right. Prison will sure as hell kill you."

"I know how to be a prisoner."

"That was fifty years ago!"

"I must take my punishment!"

"You're an old man!"

"I thought you said we were never old."

"I lied!"

"I'll be fine!"

"Are you going to be fine when some man-eater prisoner comes on to you?"

"About what?"

"Sex, stupid!"

"Nobody's going to bother an old cripple who hasn't even had an erection in fifty years."

Neither man could speak for several seconds. Their silence grew to a minute and then to two full minutes.

It was broken by Henry shouting. "I can't stand it if you do this! Don't do it, Quincy! For me, don't do it!"

Quincy grabbed his friend's two hands, which were there on the table before him. Softly, he said, "I have to, Henry."

And they continued for a while longer to speak in inter-mittment outbursts, some loud and profane, others quiet and peaceful.

Finally, Henry gave up. Quincy was going to be punished, and there was nothing Henry could do about it. As he left the room, he said in a near whisper, "I love you, Quincy Watson, even if you are a goddamn idiot."

"I love you, too, Henry—even if you aren't."

"I'll go with you to prison."

And they laughed together about that crazy idea.

·   ·   ·

Four days later, the same jury that had convicted John Quincy Watson returned a sentence of five years in prison—eighteen months of real time, assuming good behavior.

At the sentencing hearing, Watson did not make a state-ment, did not ask for mercy or sympathy, and did not permit his attorney, Henry Howell, Jr., to call any character wit-nesses.

There were no appeals.

CHAPTER TWENTY-ONE

They were awakened, as always, by the voice of a guard on a P.A. system: "Wake up, campers. Wake up and be happy. Wake up for another happy day as a guest of the tax-payers of the Golden State of California."

Watson, having slept in his white jockey undershorts, quickly slipped into the standard pair of blue jeans, blue shirt, and work shoes and walked out of his cell toward the big bathroom at the end of corridor 4. He had his cane in his right hand, his toothbrush, razor, and other toiletries in a cloth bag in the other.

He always hoped to be among the first in line, but he never was. Between his age and his lame leg, he couldn't move fast enough to beat any of the other convicts. This morning was the same as the others. There were already ten or twelve prisoners ahead of him, waiting for a turn at the commodes, sinks, and showers.

"You expecting to get used to all this, Reverend?" said the prisoner in front of him in line. He was a Hispanic, about thirty, whom Quincy had seen a few times before in the mess hall. He didn't know his name or his crime.

"Nobody smart ever gets used to this shit," said another man, black, about fifty, just behind Watson. Watson didn't remember ever seeing him before. "Particularly you special ones."

"But there are other things to do to keep the body happy," said an old white man with a flirtatious wink at Watson.

"You likin' it here in hell, Famous Preacher Man?" said someone else Watson didn't see.

Watson said nothing in response. He had said nothing to anyone about anything for the last two days. He had spoken many words out loud, but they were only for himself.

This was his thirty-ninth day at the Tom Bradley Minimum Security Correctional Institution in a sandy valley outside Bakersfield. The California newspapers, after his sentencing, had pointed out that where he was going was one of the softest of the thirty-three facilities in the state prison system. The articles described it as being more like a low-end motel than a prison.

Henry did move into a real Bakersfield motel near the prison with the idea of staying awhile and visiting regularly. But on the morning of the fourth day he woke up with a pain in his stomach, the Hyena's favorite target on his body fifty years earlier. Henry told Watson it hurt enough to justify checking it out. So he went home to Massachusetts General in Boston, where the doctors told him he had a tumor.

He e-mailed Watson at the prison about it through Henry junior's law office. His message ended with: "No tumor would dare fool with the late Henry Howell! So long for now. I'll be back soon. Meanwhile, just remember what I told you at Sengei 4—survivors survive to fight."

Watson tried to remember that.

He tried to remember that when he stood in the bathroom line in the morning. And in the lines for food, clean clothes, fresh towels and bed linens, soap and toiletries, magazines, newspapers, and mail. He tried when hot food was cold and the cold drinks were hot, when the television was on so loud in the recreation room it was impossible to read or think, when stench from unwashed bodies filled small work and study rooms and the tiny cell he shared with five other men, when the vulgarity of language and habits turned his mind and stomach, when he walked outside into the exercise yard and realized there was no exercise or game he wished to or could play.

He tried to remember that when he wanted to keep walking from his cell down corridor 4 until he was outside beyond the gate and the fence and on the road toward his San Antonio, the place made warm and comfortable by sunshine and trees and a quietly open style that he loved. He wouldn't have stopped until he was swimming laps in the pool at his house in Alamo Heights.

He had come to this prison having accepted what kind of life lay ahead for him in San Antonio and everywhere else after he served his time. He had resigned his ordination as a Methodist minister and publicly declared that he would never again preach from the pulpit of a Methodist or any other church. No one convicted of taking another's life should. That sermon at St. Luke's in San Diego before the trial had been his last.

He accepted the fact that he was now and forever a celebrity murderer in that growing lineup with O. J. Simpson, the Menendez brothers, the British au pair. He knew that to all but his closest friends, he would always be that Methodist bishop who killed an innocent Japanese businessman by cracking the man's neck with his bare hands and then, when that didn't do the trick, tossing him off a hotel balcony.

He had received several book offers from New York publishers, and agents and producers had contacted him about

the movie and television rights to his story. Watson turned
everything down, but Henry junior told him it really didn't
matter. Books and movies would be written and made any-
way about John Quincy Watson the Killer Bishop. His story
would live forever in scores of languages in the book and
video stores of the world.

The mail from strangers continued to pour into prison.
Most brought messages of support and sympathy, some in
ways he could do without. Those who hated the Japanese
laid out complicated racial theories for why the Japanese are
a naturally brutal race of people. Others urged him either to
lead a crusade for a formal Japanese apology for World War
II or to fight Japan's ongoing efforts to defeat the United
States economically in a new kind of trade and money war.
There was also hateful mail declaring him a cold-blooded
racist killer who should have been executed for what he did
to that innocent man, Bill Joe Tashimoto.

Bill Joe Tashimoto, the innocent man. It was on Watson's
twelfth day at Bakersfield that the letter about Tashimoto arrived in the day's mail. Singapore was the postmark.

It was carefully handwritten in tiny letters on heavy blue
stationery. The correspondent was a man who said he had
watched Court TV's coverage of the Watson trial every day
on Singapore television. First the Australian, now the Singaporean, thought Watson. Why is everybody in the world
watching American court trials on television?

The man wrote that during World War II he was forced as
an eleven-year-old boy to work for the Japanese as a kind of
slave houseboy for officers. He thought he recognized the
photograph of Bill Joe Tashimoto as possibly being that of a
Japanese army officer who was an interpreter-interrogator
for the various prison camps in Singapore. He got a copy of
the Tashimoto photo from the *Straits Times,* Singapore's
daily newspaper, and showed it around to several others still

alive and living in Singapore who would have known the man. All agreed it looked exactly like him.

The man wrote,

His prisoners were mostly British and Singaporean Chinese, who the Japanese particularly hated because they were viewed as Asian agents of the White Devils and as spies and potential saboteurs. The prisoners called this man "Killer Bat" because of his appearance and his behavior. He was particularly brutal to Europeans and others with white skin. White men with red hair suffered the very most, because, he said: "Those with the reddest hair have the whitest skin." But he hurt all prisoners. He burned holes in their skin with cigarettes, he filled their bodies with water and then sat on their bloated stomachs, he cut off or out parts of their bodies—livers were the favorites—and then had them cooked and served to other Japanese officers, he stuck the ends of bamboo sticks up their rectums, he hung them spread-eagled upside down in the sun for hours by their ankles, he cut off their heads with a sword he claimed was the sharpest in all of the Japanese army, he whipped them with leather whips and bamboo sticks until they died, he shot them dead in the back of the head with his pistol, he kicked them and threw them about repeatedly to keep up his martial arts skills, he used them to test the way humans react to different kinds of injuries and other traumas.

He was not the only one doing such horrible things, of course. But he was among the worst and he stood out more because of his flawless English. You have done a service, Bishop John Quincy Watson, by disposing of him. You should think of it as an execution for crimes committed rather than as murder. I hope that the people of your country, despite the court finding, will do the same. I regret very much that you were sent to prison. You should have been given a medal by the people of Singapore if not by your own people.

> With respect and honor forever,
> Pok Ka Wew
> Singapore

Watson reread the letter at least thirty times the day it came. And again the next day and the next. By then he had every word memorized. But he still carried it with him wherever he went—to meals, to the recreation room, to the exercise yard, bathroom, to study group.

Several times he went to the phone in the recreation hall intending to call somebody about the letter. Watson had use of the phone for a three-minute outgoing call every day if he wished. The prison warden, whose father was a World War II army veteran who had been wounded in the battle of Okinawa, believed Bishop Watson—no matter what he did in that hotel room in San Diego—had earned the right to special privileges in a B-29 over Japan fifty years ago. Watson was once again a special prisoner.

He thought about calling Henry, but Henry needed to be left in peace to deal with his own problem. There was no one else to call. Joyce was gone. Rick was gone. Henry junior? With the Singapore letter in his hand, Watson once began dialing Henry junior's office number in Boston. But he never hit the last digit to make the connection.

It was on that morning that he began to speak aloud only to himself. He went to the recreation room because he could do it there without being heard or disturbing anyone. The noise of the television gave him privacy.

He spoke out loud about a tearful confession of guilt he had received from young Doug Wilson shortly after the verdict and sentencing. The angry POW's son had been terribly wrong about how a jury would excuse—cheer, even—Watson's actions because of what had been done to him fifty years ago. Wilson was stunned, confused. How could they do this to you, bishop? I'm sorry. I don't understand it.

"They held me individually responsible just as we did the Hyena that night in the shed."

He spoke about the meaning of the Singapore letter. Did it really excuse what he had done? Did it make his killing of Bill Joe Tashimoto justified homicide? Heroic homicide? Good homicide? Did this prove that Henry was really right about this second Tashimoto also deserving to die?

"So, in a strange way, those eyes did not lie to me after all?"

He talked out loud about how right Henry had been about being a prisoner again. The lack of freedom and privacy, the invasion of other people's noises and smells and stupidities. The sheer awfulness of being confined and demeaned. Yes, he deserved to be punished for what he did. But this *much* punishment?

"And now, with the Singapore letter, do I still deserve this life in this place with these people?"

On this Tuesday, his thirty-ninth day, after finally getting access to a commode to eliminate his body waste, he added the letter from Singapore before flushing it all away.

Then he moved on to the dining room, where he only picked at a breakfast of runny, lukewarm scrambled eggs, two pieces of crisp bacon, a glass of warm tomato juice, and a cup of strong black coffee.

From there, he went to the regular Tuesday meeting of his study group. The usual six fellow convicts were there to talk about religion and philosophy. Watson was the discussion leader, having been recruited on arrival by the prison chaplain, an Episcopalian priest who came out from town to perform God's work on a contract basis with the state. Watson had agreed because he felt an obligation and because he decided two ninety-minute sessions a week might help his mind pass the time of imprisonment.

"Hey, Bishop, what did it feel like when you broke that little Jap's neck?" asked Terwilliger, a young white in his late twenties who had been a long-haul tractor-trailer driver. He was serving time for transporting cocaine taped to the axles of his truck on runs between Los Angeles and San Jose.

The bishop did not respond. Terwilliger, possibly the dumbest man Watson had ever known, had asked that question at the beginning of every session. Usually, Watson gave him some kind of answer. Not this morning.

"I have a question about believing in Jesus Christ," said Lawrence, a black man who seemed to be among the quickest of the prisoners Watson had come across thus far. He had been a Ford-dealership accountant in his thirties who got caught stealing from his bosses in Oakland.

Watson said nothing.

"I was always told that if you do good things but you don't do them in Jesus' name, then they don't count for much," said Lawrence. "Do you believe that, Quincy?"

"Quincy." Watson had told everyone to call him by his given name but because of his age and celebrity, few did. Lawrence was one of the few, and every time he did, it jarred Watson to realize that he was on a first-name basis with convicted felons.

Again Watson did not respond.

The seven men, all dressed identically in blue denim, were seated in school-style desk chairs arranged in a circle in the center of a small room near the main recreation area. There was a doorway but no door.

"You not talking today, Preacher?" one of the others asked.

Watson shook his head.

"So what do we do?" Lawrence asked.

Watson closed his eyes and lowered his head.

"You're not shutting down already, are you?" Watson didn't look up to see who'd asked the question. It sounded like Ippolito, a slick Italian in his sixties serving two years for bilking some old Armenian ladies in Fresno out of their money.

"Well, let's go on and talk without him," said someone who sounded like Lawrence.

They talked—mostly about a new California correction policy on dress and grooming. Every prisoner in the system was to be issued white uniforms with CDC PRISONER printed on the back. All prisoners will have to cut their hair, shave their beards, quit wearing earrings, and stop lifting weights. The policy, said officials, was necessary for public safety and for the maintenance of discipline and good order.

The study group thought otherwise, and they debated how to make their feelings known—go on a hunger strike, burn a few mattresses, take a few guards hostage? Not another word was spoken about religion or philosophy.

And at no time did Watson do anything other than sit silently, slumped in his seat with his head down and his eyes, ears, and mind closed.

The others left him there that way ninety minutes later, when the session ended. A guard came in after a while and rousted him to go to lunch. Watson went to the dining room, got in the cafeteria line with a tray, and took a plate of macaroni and cheese, a thin slice of cold ham, some green beans, a bowl of apple cobbler, and a small glass of sweetened iced tea. He took some silverware wrapped in a white paper napkin and sat down at a table with seven other prisoners.

A few inmates tried to talk to him, but he said nothing and barely even looked at them. He ate a few bites of food and took a sip or two of the tea.

Watson did not go to pick up his mail as he had done immediately after lunch the first thirty-eight days. He went instead to the recreation room to talk to himself out loud again. *The Joanie Wilson Show,* exploring the pros and cons of adopting the children of drug-addicted prostitutes from Southeast Asia, was blaring from all three large TV sets. The room, large and open like a hotel lobby, was filled with haphazardly arranged vinyl institutional-style chairs in various shades of blue, small walnut writing tables, a couple of Ping-Pong tables, and a table holding stacks of paperback novels.

Watson went to a corner chair, sat down, and faced the pastel blue wall. Other prisoners were sitting close by, but there was no way they'd be able to hear what he was going to say to himself.

He opened his mouth to speak but said nothing. His body started quivering.

So Watson closed his mouth and stopped trying to talk out loud—and the quivering stopped.

He sat there silently for three hours, hearing but not listening to or watching the television. A western starring Jimmy Stewart and Richard Widmark followed the talk show. All Watson picked up about the movie was that Stewart was a good guy and Widmark wasn't. During a news break he heard that the consumer price index was down and that meant Federal Reserve chairman Alan Greenspan probably wouldn't be raising interest rates anytime soon.

"You're fading faster'n any I ever saw," an inmate said to him later outside in the exercise yard. Watson paid little attention to him.

He also remained mute and unresponsive at supper—chili over spaghetti, a tomato salad, chocolate cake with white icing, and unsweetened iced tea—and later back in the recreation room for more television watching. All Watson heard this time were the TV studio audiences laughing.

When he went back to his cell shortly after nine o'clock, he did so without saying anything to anyone. He didn't stop by the bathroom, and he lay down on his bed without taking off his clothes or shoes.

Then he closed his eyes and said a prayer to himself, saying aloud only the last line—"I pray the Lord my soul to take."

.   .   .

When six o'clock came the morning of his fortieth day as a prisoner, everything began again as it had on the thirty-ninth. The loud voice of a guard announced the day had arrived.

But this time John Quincy Watson did not stir. He did not get out of bed and move as fast as he could to the bathroom. The five other prisoners in the cell let him sleep. They paid him no mind as they went about their routines.

It wasn't until just before eight o'clock that two guards came back down corridor 4 looking for Watson. They found him still in bed, eyes closed, lying on his back, his hands folded on his chest as if he were praying, his mouth set in a soft smile. His cane was on the bed next to him.

"Hey, Bishop!" yelled one of the guards. "This ain't The Four Seasons—up and at 'em!"

The bishop didn't move. The other guard moved over to the bed. "He looks sick or something," he said to his colleague.

The first guard came over. "You smell what I smell?" he asked. "He's more than sick."

They both shook Watson. No eyes opened, no sound came.

The second guard picked up Watson's left arm and felt the wrist for a pulse. In a few seconds, he put the wrist back down. "Yeah. The old son of a bitch is dead."

The other ran down the corridor to spread the news.

The guard who remained looked hard at Watson's smile and then at the rest of his face and on down his front to his feet. He turned the body to one side and then to another, searching for blood or some sign of violence.

There wasn't a mark on him.

ACKNOWLEDGMENTS

I wish to thank Annette Miller, Sandi Fox, Stuart Taylor, Judy Willis, Dr. Roy Rubenfeld, and my brother, the Rev. Fred Lehrer, for research assistance in the writing of this book. I would also like to thank my editor, Susanna Porter, and my copy editor, Margaret Wimberger.

J.L.

ABOUT THE AUTHOR

JIM LEHRER is the author of many books and plays and is the executive editor/anchor of *The NewsHour with Jim Lehrer* on PBS. He was a 1999 recipient of a National Humanities Award for his writing and journalism. He lives in Washington, D.C.

PublicAffairs is a new publishing house and a tribute to the standards, values, and flair of three persons who have served as mentors to countless reporters, writers, editors, and book people of all kinds, including me.

I. F. Stone, proprietor of *I. F. Stone's Weekly*, combined a commitment to the First Amendment with entrepreneurial zeal and reporting skill and became one of the great independent journalists in American history. At the age of eighty, Izzy published *The Trial of Socrates*, which was a national bestseller. He wrote the book after he taught himself ancient Greek.

Benjamin C. Bradlee was for nearly thirty years the charismatic editorial leader of *The Washington Post*. It was Ben who gave the *Post* the range and courage to pursue such historic issues as Watergate. He supported his reporters with a tenacity that made them fearless, and it is no accident that so many became authors of influential, best-selling books.

Robert L. Bernstein, the chief executive of Random House for more than a quarter century, guided one of the nation's premier publishing houses. Bob was personally responsible for many books of political dissent and argument that challenged tyranny around the globe. He is also the founder and was the longtime chair of Human Rights Watch, one of the most respected human rights organizations in the world.

.   .   .

For fifty years, the banner of Public Affairs Press was carried by its owner Morris B. Schnapper, who published Gandhi, Nasser, Toynbee, Truman, and about 1,500 other authors. In 1983 Schnapper was described by *The Washington Post* as "a redoubtable gadfly." His legacy will endure in the books to come.

Peter Osnos, *Publisher*